Books by/Libros por JP Greene

The Arid Road Home - Wilderwest Press 2022
The Beauty of Sadness - Word Rebels Press 2022
Meet Me Between Breaths - Tape Publishing 2025
Tormenta - Tape Publishing 2025

Serie Poesía de Any Pascual

Sensibilidad: Los poemas de una Adolescente Altamente Sensible - 2022
Un año en versos: Poema diario - 2024
Antología 8M: Letras Unidas - 2024
Cuevas y bosques: Poesía natural - 2024

Poetry Series by Any Pascual

Sensitivity: Poems of a Highly Sensitive Teenager - 2023
A year in verses: Poem diary - 2024
Caves and forests: Natural Poetry - 2024
Verses till midnight: Cozy poetry book - 2025

¿De dónde has salido?
él le preguntó.

De tus mejores sueños, dijo ella.
He venido a rescatarte.

Or destrozarme.

Bueno, lo uno o lo otro, dijo ella.
Y entonces se fue.

Where did you even come from,
he asked her.

Your wildest dreams, she said. I've
come to rescue you.

Or wreck me.

Well, one or the other, she said.
And then she was gone.

Tormenta

Una tranquila playa mexicana. El mar implacable.
Un amor sin piedad.

por JP Greene
traducción por Any Pascual

Tormenta

A quiet Mexican beach. The relentless sea.
A love without mercy.

by JP Greene
translated by Any Pascual

TORMENTA
Una tranquila playa mexicana. El mar implacable. Un amor sin piedad.

por JP Greene
Traducción por Any Pascual

Copyright © 2025 Joshua Paul Greene
Traducción al español © 2026 Joshua Paul Greene

Publicado por Tape Publishing, 2026

Este libro fue escrito en 11 puntos en la fuente Goudy Old Style.

10 9 8 7 6 5 4 3 2

Impreso en papel libre de ácido. Para más información, escribe a rep@tapepub.com

Fotografía de portada, diseño y maquetación por JP Greene y Tape Publishing.
Library of Congress numero de control: 2026907246

ISBN – 979-8-9913038-3-5
Tapa blanda – Edición bilingüe.

NOTA DEL EDITOR:

TORMENTA
A quiet Mexican beach. The relentless sea. A love without mercy.

by JP Greene
Translation by Any Pascual

Copyright © 2025 Joshua Paul Greene
Spanish translation © 2026 Joshua Paul Greene

Published by Tape Publishing, 2026

This book was set in 11 pt Goudy Old Style font.

10 9 8 7 6 5 4 3 2

Printed on acid-free paper. For information write to rep@tapepub.com

Cover photography, design and book layout by JP Greene and Tape Publishing.
Library of Congress Control Number: 2026907246

ISBN – 979-8-9913038-3-5
Paperback – Dual-Language Edition

PUBLISHER'S NOTE:

Para mis hijos, que estaban
conmigo cuando esta historia se
concibió en Sayulita, México.

For my kids, who were with me
when this story was conceived in
Sayulita, Mexico.

Nota de la Traductora

Dicen que no hay que conocer a tus ídolos. Yo me alegro de haberlo hecho, porque JP Greene y esta historia de amor en vacaciones han cambiado mi vida.

Admiro al autor desde un día lluvioso en el que leí por primera vez una de sus breves notas de amor escritas a máquina. Su voz llegó a mi vida y ya no se fue. Todo lo que escribe me toca el alma, y me siento muy honrada y agradecida de que me eligiera como su traductora para Tormenta, una historia que me conquistó desde que se anunció su primera edición en inglés.

Al traducir la novela, he podido conocer a estos personajes, disfrutar y emocionarme con ellos, y he vivido mi propio viaje interior mientras traducía el suyo. Siento que soy mejor persona (y escritora) gracias a todo lo que Damian y Emilia me han enseñado, sobre su mundo y también sobre el nuestro. Ya casi no puedo imaginar mi vida sin ellos, y creo sinceramente que esta historia es más necesaria hoy que nunca.

Gracias a Tormenta, he redescubierto mi lengua materna y me he vuelto a enamorar de todos los matices que el español ofrece a la literatura y, en especial, a las historias de amor. En un mundo donde los libros se consumen deprisa, Tormenta nos anima a disfrutar de cada momento y a vivir intensamente, sin pedir permiso. A prestar atención, reflexionar y releer para que no se acabe nunca. Y sobre todo, a dejar que el amor nos sorprenda.

Aunque soy española, México es un país que llevo en mi corazón desde mi adolescencia. Todos los que me conocen saben que es mi lugar favorito en el mundo. Traducir este libro me ha permitido viajar mentalmente a Sayulita, caminar por sus calles, visitar sus tiendas y disfrutar de sus paisajes, especialmente su playa y su mar. ¡Y qué decir de su gente! Es una experiencia que nunca olvidaré. ¡Viva México!

En estas páginas encontrarás pasión, profundidad, una pizca de locura y una libertad que cautiva como la brisa marina. Y quizás, como me ha ocurrido a mí, descubras un hogar íntimo y honesto al que volver de vacaciones una y otra vez.

Te doy la bienvenida a Tormenta. Vamos, pasa la página.

- Any Pascual, poeta y traductora, febrero de 2026.

Translator's Note

They say you shouldn't meet your idols. I'm glad I did, because JP Greene and this vacation romance story have changed my life.

I've admired the author since a rainy day when I first read one of his short typewritten love notes. His voice entered my life and never left. Everything he writes touches my soul, and I feel very honored and grateful that he chose me as his translator for Tormenta, a story that won me over from the moment its first edition in English was announced.

In translating the novel, I have been able to get to know these characters, enjoy and get excited with them, and I have lived my own inner journey while translating theirs. I feel that I am a better person (and writer) thanks to everything Damian and Emilia have taught me, about their world and also about ours. I can hardly imagine my life without them now, and I sincerely believe that this story is more necessary today than ever.

Thanks to Tormenta, I have rediscovered my mother tongue and fallen in love again with all the nuances that Spanish offers to literature and, in particular, to love stories. In a world where books are consumed quickly, Tormenta encourages us to enjoy every moment and live intensely, without asking permission. To pay attention, reflect, and reread so that it never ends. And above all, to let love surprise us.

Although I am Spanish, Mexico is a country that has been in my heart since my adolescence. Everyone who knows me knows that it is my favorite place in the world. Translating this book has allowed me to travel mentally to Sayulita, walk its streets, visit its shops, and enjoy its landscapes, especially its beach and sea. And what can I say about its people! It is an experience I will never forget. Viva Mexico!

In these pages you will find passion, depth, a touch of madness, and a freedom that captivates like the sea breeze. And perhaps, as has happened to me, you will discover an intimate and honest home to return to again and again on vacation.

I welcome you to Tormenta. Come on, turn the page.

- Any Pascual, poet and translator, February 2026.

Tormenta

English

La Playa

He opened the book and the first thing he noticed was the slip of receipt paper twenty pages in from the last time he'd started reading it. How many years ago had that been? Probably the last time he'd taken a vacation. That figured. Two years now? Five? A cloud shifted in the sky and the page darkened and he heard the sound of waves crashing and he realized he couldn't see the page with his sunglasses on now that the sky had changed. He took them off and positioned them on the top of his head. Pulled the bookmark from its place and put it farther back, intent on reading past page twenty this time. People read books on vacations, right? He was one of those people, he'd decided. A long time ago. Had always been one of those people. Some people read all the time. Who's got time for that? But during vacation – for leisure. To read would be a pleasure.

He refocused and read the first page. It was a thin paperback he'd found in one of those curbside libraries near the beach. On his last vacation, he remembers. Hemingway – The Old Man and the Sea. It bent and twisted in the slight breeze, the pages fluttering up beneath his thumb. Faint sound of rustling paper. How nice. He could smell the ocean – the actual ocean out beyond the beach. The sand beneath him was warm on his toes where they hung off the edge of the beach towel. He could smell the sea, and he liked it. The salt, and the slight oceanic smell. What was that? What made it smell like that? Fainter here than other places. Seattle, for example – he'd been there and the ocean smelled ancient and deep and somehow more pungent than this sea. And he was closer here. Maybe it was not so much the ocean itself in Seattle but the port. The town. That was probably it. He sniffed deeply, and returned to the page.

The clouds shifted again and the page shone as though backlit in the bright clean light and he squinted at it for a moment trying to go on reading – intent on avoiding distractions. God damn that's bright, he thought. He slid his sunglasses back on. There was a smudge in the corner. He ignored it for a moment and then he tented the book over his thigh and found his shirt among his things beside him and pulled off the glasses and cleaned them to his satisfaction and then put them back on and then picked back up the book. This is why I never read, he thought. Jesus Christ.

A wave broke and some children playing in the ocean squealed. Yelled at each other in Spanish. He couldn't understand them. Not really. A phrase here or there he recognized. Childish inflection over simple words. Something about their enthusiasm caught his attention, made him smile, staring softly in their direction without really seeing. That sound was something – the sound of the waves. The ocean alive, almost. There was the growing static of the wave and then the crest and the crash like some great release, and their voices – the voices of the children – gaining as he imagined the great bluegreen bell of the wave rising from the surface and folding over itself and then he imagined it breaking over their heads as they laughed overwhelmed with joy, the ocean powerful beyond their comprehension but gentle with them. Kind, the ocean. And at other times merciless and awful. He returned to his reading.

It was a slow book to start. Not much of a book at all, really, at least in terms of length – it had been bold of Hemingway to start a short book so slowly. Or maybe he was just not a very good reader. He'd heard that before – that some people just don't have the immediate comprehension or the attention span or the attentiveness to detail to take pleasure from reading. He was enjoying the book. What did that mean? How often people escape the confines of their supposed boxes. He wasn't sure though, honestly, if he was enjoying the book, or just enjoying the act of reading. Of being on the beach and reading. The clouds had fully dispersed now and the sun was bright overhead and he'd gotten comfortable on the towel finally and he was warm and the air smelled nice and he could see how someone – someone who read a lot – could take great pleasure in something like this. In this exact thing, he thought. This was it. This was reading. He realized he'd lost his place on the page – had been reading without actually reading – and he backtracked and found where he'd lost his focus and then he picked it back up.

An old man and a boy talking. The boy very kind and the old man, too. They don't have relationships like that anymore, he thought. Maybe not in America. Maybe in Mexico? In Cuba where the book took place. How similar, he wondered, was Cuba to Mexico. He liked Mexico. The children were still in the waves playing and laughing. He noticed the head of a woman in the water, too, bobbing up and down with the waves. Off a ways from the children – not with them, he thought to himself. Not their mother, probably. None of the children called out to her.

She'd been floating on her back, but had bobbed up when he'd happened to look out. He thought that maybe she had looked his way, had maybe held his gaze. Probably not – probably she hadn't seen him anyway. He imagined that she was very beautiful – imagining because she was too far for him to truly see. But it felt as if she was very beautiful. What a weird projection, he thought. Of course you would think that. She turned, her black hair shining in the sun, and faced toward the open ocean. Her image slightly obscured by ripples of heat in the atmosphere. By the reflection of the sun off the surface of the water, like flashbulbs in old film clips of famous concerts, or like fireflies. He noticed himself smiling, staring blankly at the page. He checked the page number. Twenty-six – that was better than the last time. A boy came by and asked if he wanted to buy some camarones on a stick. He assessed that they were shrimp and guessed that they had been marinated and grilled, and they were orange and good-looking in the bright sun. Blonde beach, deep turquoise ocean, orange shrimp and the green of the lime atop the shrimp on the skewer. Beyond the boy selling the shrimp, in soft focus, the head of the woman he'd seen, hair black and resplendent in the sun. He asked if the shrimp were spicy, trying to remember the Spanish word for it. Estas caliente? he asked. The boy laughed good-naturedly. Spicy? he asked. He felt like he might have blushed, and nodded. No really, unless you want, the boy responded in broken English, holding up a bottle of hot sauce. Un poquito, the man said, making a pinching motion with his fingers. The boy nodded gravely, as though the matter of the spice was very serious. The man asked how much. Forty, the boy said, or three for a hundred pesos. That's what, he thought to himself. Two bucks. Or three for five. He nodded, dug through his pocket, produced a few bills and handed them over and the boy pocketed the money and drizzled some hot sauce on each of the shrimp on the skewer, then handed it down to him where he sat on the beach. He thanked the man and then continued to the next person on the beach, the same interaction repeated again as though some fold in time had produced the same scenario but with one actor different. He smelled the skewered shrimp and closed his eyes it smelled so good. He squeezed the lime over them, leaning his arm and the skewer over the sand so as not to drip on his towel, and then he ate them and he found that they were in fact very, very good. He looked for the boy once he'd eaten them all, thinking he might buy two more after all, but the boy was gone. As his eyes returned from scanning down the beach he saw her coming out of the water.

The woman from before. She was walking up out of the water. He was stilled, watching her. He'd practiced not staring at women, every time he'd seen a very beautiful one. He had intentionally practiced the act of not gawking. A glance was forgivable, but to stare – that was piggish. It was rude, and objectifying. He was not that sort of person. He had friends that were that way, and they disgusted him. But with her, he couldn't help himself. And she stared back. Coming out of the water, faintly smiling; at first she had had her eyes closed, her hands pressing back the water out of her hair, droplets of water forming on her skin and running in rivulets down her body, and he felt so jealous of the water for that brief instant and then instantly shameful for such an intrusive thought – intrusive the thought felt into her own personal space, her own body. She'd pressed the water back off of her hair and he'd watched her and her eyes were closed like she was savoring the way the sun enveloped her, sun and water competing for her. To touch her. And his eyes, thrust somehow into this battle. And where was she? In the middle, and loving it. Yes, he got the impression somehow that she loved being the prize in some sense. Or maybe it was just that she loved the harmony she felt with everything around her. God, what was happening in his mind, he wondered. And then she was opening her eyes, slowly, savoringly, her hips moving as she walked effortlessly out of the water, her height gaining as she stepped higher onto the beach. Her eyes were opening and then she saw him looking and she smiled and did not break his gaze for what felt like an actual eternity. She walked, and walked, and walked toward him, and he watched and watched and watched and she looked at him like she already loved him and then she walked past him and he had not moved his head but he had followed her with his eyes. He was trying to decide whether to turn around and see where she'd gone, but had as of yet been unable to bring himself to do it when her voice, it must've been her voice, said casually: Is that The Old Man and the Sea?

He looked at the book still held open in his hands – what had his hands been doing this whole time? Apparently nothing – and nodded. He was about to speak when she appeared beside him and began to sit down beside his towel. Awkwardly, suddenly, like a subject making way for a queen, he lurched sideways, as if in deference, as if out of respect for her very aura, and managed to offer her a space on the towel. She laughed good-naturedly and sat in the sand. He could not avoid looking at the way the sand clung to the bare skin on the backs of her thighs. The sand, now in the mix, too – sand, sun, water, his gaze, what a lineup. I love that book, she said then, squeezing the rest of the water from the ends of her long, black hair. He realized then how long her hair was. Down nearly to the middle of her back. Not that she was tall. But it was a lot of hair and it was incredibly beautiful. Her eyes, too. Jesus Christ, he thought. Don't look too closely, you'll never recover. And here she was sitting and talking to him.

I haven't gotten very far, he said then, looking down as if remembering for the first time since she had appeared that he had the book at all. It's not a hard read or anything, I just...

I can't ever read at the beach, she said without waiting for him to finish. She had her knees up and her elbows wrapped around them, leaning forward in a relaxed sort of way, like she was about to eat a juicy piece of fruit and didn't want it dripping on her lap. She was looking out at the ocean, the sand clinging to her upper thighs where she'd sat at first. It wasn't a very ladylike way to sit, but there was something perfect about it. About her. You're just getting sentimental because she's a pretty girl giving you attention, he told himself. No, he thought then, she was perfect. Why don't you read at the beach? he asked.

I just can't, she said, moving her gaze from the horizon to meet his own eyes. She was smiling. A mischievous, knowing smile. Too much to see, to feel, I guess.

Too much to feel?

She laughed kindly, lightly. Yes – don't you think so? She ran her fingers through the sand and told him she found the beach so sensual. Just, she specified, so stimulating for the senses, you know? I don't know if I'm using the right words. I don't always know the right words in English, she said. He thought he detected a sense of embarrassment in her voice when she said this.

I know what you mean, he said. To be honest I think I've been a bit distracted myself.

Oh? she asked, raising an eyebrow. Anything in particular?

Is she flirting with me, he wondered. Well, you, for one, he said aloud and then wondered why he'd said it.

Hm, she said without hesitating even for a second, am I a good distraction, or a bad one? She was looking at him directly now. How could she be so relaxed, he thought.

He felt hot all over. He managed a chuckle. I guess we'll have to find out, he said. Where had that come from, he wondered. What was she doing to him. He never talked like this.

She let a glorious, ringing, easy laugh fall from her lips. Laughed up at the sky and the sky laughed back. How did she do that? Well, she said then, we will see. Where do you come from?

He hesitated, and he didn't know why. America, he said. Idaho.

Idaho, she asked. Oh there are potatoes there, no?

Hey, he said, more than potatoes. Lots of mountains and forests and lakes. It's really beautiful. But not like this.

No, she said. I imagine not. This is something here. This beach might be my favorite place in the world. It's a big risk for me, you know. Talking to you here. In this of all places. What if you ruin it for me?

I would never, he said.

No, she said almost wistfully. Not on purpose. But I'm your distraction, and you're my risk, I suppose. How exciting. She made a face like she had just learned a secret that made her happy.

What's your name?

Emilia, she replied. And you?

Damian, he said then. Mucho gusto, she said, extended her hand and he sat up slightly to take it in his. Good to meet you, he replied. And you live here?

She nodded. For a few years now. Not forever, probably. But for now, it's good.

Where else would you go?

Hmm... She ran her fingers through the sand on either side of her, brushing circles in the arc of the reach of her arms, like wings, or petals opening outward from where she sat. Well, before I was in Lisbon, in Portugal. I have spent some time on Malta. And in Bali. I don't know – nowhere in particular comes to mind right now. But surely there will be somewhere else. Who knows what draws us forward in our lives, you know?

He said he had usually felt like there was a lot of predetermination in his life, and asked her if she didn't have some sort of plan for what she wanted.

A plan, she asked, raising her eyebrows. She asked it as though it were a ridiculous question. As if no one in their right mind would put structure around a life. No, no plan. What would be the point? Do plans ever work out anyway? And a life is so short!

Sometimes they do, he said. Plans, I mean. For me anyway.

Well, I'm happy for you, she replied after a moment. So tell me, what plans have worked for you? I'm very curious.

It was the sort of thing that could've sounded accusatory or belittling or speculative but it did not sound that way coming from her lips. She was, entirely, as she said, curious.

I mean, I went to school for business, which was planned, and have managed to make a fairly good life for myself with my work.

She watched him, listening.

I'm a business consultant, he added without being asked. I help take businesses that don't function well, and I sort of fix them. That sounds arrogant but I don't mean it to. It's not like I'm some miracle worker. Actually, mostly what I do is help people make plans. He chuckled then, at the coincidence and the course of the conversation. What do you do for work?

I am an artist. I do tattoos.

He stared at her for a moment. As though waiting for her to go on. To say more. To add to it. But he realized that was all she was going to say about it.

And you make enough to live on with that?

She laughed that bright easy laugh again. Yes, I do. She pushed his shoulder playfully and when her hand touched his skin he felt a surge of elation, like the first draw on a cigarette.

Did you do your own tattoos, he asked.

Some, she said. I did my legs. Some others here and there. But the rest have been done by friends, other artists. It is very difficult to tattoo one's own back.

He felt silly for asking. Well I like them all, he said.

Thank you, she said, tucking a strand of hair behind her ear.

Do you have any tattoos? she asked.

No, he said. I've always worried I wouldn't like them later.

Ah, Damian, the planner, she said affectionately. He wondered if she was this familiar with everyone she met. This friendly. You should let me tattoo you, she said.

He thought of it, instantly, like a flash of an idea, he lying there on his back, or on his stomach, she with her tools producing her art on the canvas of his body. He smiled, but didn't respond. He would let her, if it came to that.

How did you become a tattooist, he asked.

My boyfriend many years ago was a tattooist. He did some of these – here she motioned to her arms – below the elbow, and my hands. He did all traditional tattoos. This was in Bali. So these are all done with a bamboo needle and natural ink, one poke at a time. There was a whole ritual around it, it's a very sacred practice there, you know.

As she spoke about this she seemed to grow sentimental. She paused.

Anyway, I became fascinated, and being an artist already for a long time, I considered it just another type of art, but on a living canvas. Like making sand drawings, almost. But longer lasting. To be honest I was very in love with him, and was interested in everything that interested him, so it is not so surprising that I wanted to learn. Thankfully he taught me very well, and I was fairly good at it, and he gave his blessing when I left to continue on with the practice on my own, even though we were separating.

Why did you break up?

Oh, I don't think of it that way. Just that we were together and then had to go apart. It was time for me to move. I could just feel it in my bones. And he understood – told me I should go actually.

Here she smiled and pulled her hair over her shoulder.

I have been very fortunate to know some very good men.

That's not something you hear every day.

No? she asked, seeming genuinely surprised.

Ha, yeah no – I feel like most of what I hear is horror stories about men being pigs.

Do you think men are pigs? Not you, obviously.

No, I don't think men are pigs. Some of us, yes. But not everyone.

Do you swim? she asked after a short lapse of silence.

I mean, do I know how to swim? he asked in response.

Well I assumed you can swim, though maybe I shouldn't? I mean to ask you if you would like to come swim with me? I'm getting overheated sitting here on the beach. Drying out like a lizard.

She stood up and brushed the backs of her thighs off, the sand falling like a fine rain, slowly and somehow cinematic. He watched. Well, she said, wrapping her hair up to the top of her head. Are you coming?

He smiled. I was kind of trying to read, he said teasingly.

Fine, she said, suit yourself. And she turned and began walking toward the water. He had the sudden urge to run after her, to tackle her into the water, or to pick her up and carry her out into the waves. He imagined what her weight would feel like in his arms. And then he put the receipt paper in the page that had been held by his finger through all that meandering conversation, and set the book on the towel, and removed his sunglasses and put them there as well, and then he ran after her, but instead of taking her into his arms he ran past her and dove head-first into the waves ahead of her. As he passed, he heard her laugh, just before the water enclosed him.

It was warmer than he had supposed it might be. Not hot, but not shockingly cold as he had expected, and the currents beneath the waves pulled him pleasurably, exerting their force gently upon his arms and legs. When he broke the surface he shook the hair from his face and wiped his eyes and almost before he could see her coming, she was lunging at him pushing him back into the oncoming wave, down beneath the water, her skin now so much on him and her arms around his waist and the water around them and he thought in some impossibly quick succession of instantaneous thought that he would have liked to die in just that way, with her arms around him, surrounded by the cool salty water, and then they came up for air, both gasping, laughing, her head thrown back in triumphant joy.

The water is perfect, he said.

I know, I could become a fish and live here forever. She floated up to lie on her back on the surface and sent a narrow stream of water from her pursed lips, like a small fountain. It arced above her face and landed in the water over her head. He thought how easily she floated there. As though she was the beneficiary of every one of nature's generosities.

You can see how flattering it is that I came out of this water to talk to you, she said then.

To talk to me?

Yes, of course.

Why?

I wanted to.

But why?

What do you mean why? Because I wanted to.

He smiled, and caught her peeking at him from the corner of her eye where she lay floating beside him. She quickly shut her eyes, smiling mischievously when they caught each other's gaze.

For a while they swam or floated or drifted with the rise and fall of the waves, enjoying the ocean in silence together. He mostly stood, submerged from the neck down, in the constantly shifting water, watching it spray up on the rocks down the beach that reached out into the surf, or allowing himself to be pulled up over the waves before they broke, looking out at the horizon line, at the endless ocean that stretched, it seemed, to the very edge of the earth, though truth be told if that were the end of the earth it would have been very small. He found the thought comforting. To be held within something so large, to be held so gently, to be moved around and to allow himself to be moved by it. He saw from the corner of his eye that she was swimming up to him. Froglike strokes of her arms and legs and a smile upon her face. And then she turned so that her back was to him and she pressed her body against his, her hands reaching behind and adhering herself to him in the currented ocean. He put his hands on her hips, and then on her stomach, the tips of his fingers resting just softly on the fabric of her swimsuit bottoms. He felt the hard fin of her hipbones, thought he felt vaguely the raised topography made by the bold lines of her tattoos, and felt some modicum of peace in the pressure of her body against his. Warm, even enveloped in the water, and the smell of the salt in her hair, which she had taken down, and now pulled over her shoulder. She lay her head back against his chest, the crown of her head falling below his collarbones, his arms wrapping her. I think I've decided that you're a very good distraction, he said.

He felt – yes, somehow felt, the thought occurred to him – her smile as he said this. Nuzzle somehow closer to him, maybe the slight tilt of her hips into him, the slight arch in her back that her shoulders might press more fully against the wet skin of his chest. And maybe he pressed slightly into her hips with his own, his right hand on the low flat of her stomach, his left hand on her pelvis, and he pulling her toward him. She looked up at him then, without turning around, craned her neck to see, and he looked down and he kissed her. Or she kissed him, the two of them kissing each other in the water, and the waves rocking them.

They stayed for a long time in this proximity, though their shape changed here and there, but it seemed as if they must continue to be touching. That it had somehow become very important to them both. And when they went in it was with her walking in front and leading him by the hand and she spread her blanket on the sand and they laid down together, side by side, facing one another, he propped up on one arm, his top hand on the rise of her hip, her top leg between his at the knee, she laying on one folded arm, her hair like a pillow beneath her. He brushed an errant strand behind her ear. Maybe they talked, or perhaps just looked at one another, kissing occasionally, the salt on her lips, the soft warmth of her tongue where it darted against his. The men came and cleared the umbrellas and chairs from the beach at five in the evening and Damian and Emilia ran out into the waves once again, their blanket – yes, their blanket, he thought, his and hers together – there alone on the broad beach and the palms and other flora rising in a dense brush behind, and the two of them in the water.

La Cena

They had both wanted to shower before they went for dinner, and so they went to her home and did this together. She thought they might make love there in the shower but besides touching her and kissing her and very clearly watching the way she moved, no longer questioning the ethics of watching her – thank God, she thought – he did not try to make love to her, even though he did become slightly aroused while their bodies brushed against each other under the cool running water. She rubbed soap over his back and massaged his shoulders and he let his head rest forward on the stone of the wall and she could feel him relax under her fingers. They kissed under the running water, her body pressed against his, his hands on either side of her face, her hands on his hips. Fuck, I want you, he said, and she started to touch him, but he stopped her. No, he said. Not yet.

After the shower as they dried off in the tiny bathroom, she offered to rinse his clothes and said they could lie in bed while waiting for them to dry a bit on the line. He said he was hungry and wanted a drink, and anyway his Airbnb was on the way into town and they could stop in on their way for him to change.

He watched her get dressed, and she was aware of and enjoyed his eyes upon her as she lightly applied her eyeliner and the smallest bit of mascara and some natural-looking lipstick. Slightly redder than her natural lips. Subtle, which she thought was funny because she didn't really consider herself to be very subtle at all. As she did all of this in the mirror, naked, the towel wrapped around her hair, standing on her tiptoes to lean toward the mirror, she thought about his reluctance to go to bed with her. Or his composure. Which was it, she wondered. Was it something about her body, now that he'd seen it? It probably wasn't that. She couldn't help but wonder. Maybe he was religious. Maybe he just actually had strict rules for himself and she was foolish to think that just because she was beautiful he would break them for her. She wanted him to break his rules for her, but also she thrilled at the idea that she could test him and he would not give in. It tortured her in a way, for him to have turned her down. He hadn't though, she knew. But it felt that way, in a playful, teasing sort of way that served only, for her, to increase the tension, the desire, the wanting. A kind of power he now had over her.

Yes, she wanted him more for wanting her and not taking her the first chance he'd had. How many men she'd swam with had tried to finger her in the water? She felt her desire and his restraint like a small dull ache in her lower abdomen, a warmth between her legs. All the while he sat against her headboard, naked himself, but wrapped in a towel that he not get her bed wet with his swimming trunks while he waited. He watched her the entire time she got ready, and she was careful to stay fully in his view. Once she had finished at the mirror, she dropped the towel from around her hair, leaving it in a pile on the bathroom floor, and walked into her room, naked and her hair damp still but no longer dripping, hanging down her back. She went through a few garments and took several dresses off of their hangers but decided against them and left them, too, on the floor in front of the built-in closet. He watched her all the while, and after she had gone through much of the closet she asked him to choose between an off-white crocheted top that showed most of her stomach, with a long olive-green skirt, or a thin black dress that tied around the back of her neck. The back was cut low, almost to the absolute bottom of her lower back, the bottom hem falling to her mid-thigh, and loose, the skirt, so that it would spin out when she twirled. She felt almost alarmingly sensual in this dress, and it was carefully that she chose the occasions on which to wear it. In particular, she liked to catch glimpses of her reflection in windows, or mirrors, the way her back looked, exposed, arching, and the way her legs looked coming from beneath the skirt. She knew which one she wanted to wear, but she wanted to test him in his motives, maybe, or maybe she just wanted to give him the opportunity to participate in her dressing, as she hoped that maybe he'd come to feel some propriety over her and take into his own hands her undressing as well.

He chose the black dress, which made her very happy in an almost overwhelming sort of way. She put it on for him and he stood behind her and helped her tie it behind her neck – her idea, even though she had done it herself every other time – and then she stood back, letting him admire her. Inviting him to admire her. She spun, and felt the rush of air as the skirt lifted and felt the thrill of wearing a dress like that with very little on underneath. She thought that maybe he would let his hand touch her thigh over dinner. That maybe he would take her in the dress when they got home – how easy that would be. She could wrap his neck and he could pick her up and hold her and there would be very little left between them at all. She almost shivered thinking about it. What do you think, she asked, ending her twirl and facing him.

You look incredibly beautiful, he said, smiling. He seemed unphased. Interested, of course, obviously attracted, but not out of his mind. It unnerved and excited her. He took his damp swimming suit from the door handle where it had been hung and walked by her, kissing her forehead as he passed, wrapped still in his towel, and closed the bathroom door behind himself.

When he emerged a moment later he was wearing his swimming suit again, and she thought it both somehow endearing and simultaneously frustrating that he'd concealed himself in order to change back into his shorts. He challenged her in a way she hadn't ever experienced before. Like they were old lovers, like she was his girl – his girl – but also like they were only friends. She was not accustomed to wanting to be able to classify things. She preferred to let them play out as they were meant to. But here she was, confused, turned on, excitingly frustrated. She wanted to scream and giggle and fuck. She wanted to fuck him so badly. Should we go? he asked, placing his hand on the small of her back. She nodded, and he led the way from her house.

When they arrived at his for him to change, he invited her in, but she felt as if she should wait in the living room while he got dressed. He did not ask her what he should wear. He did not look through his things to decide what to put on. She hadn't expected him to. When he returned to her just a minute or two later, he was wearing a pair of well-fitted jeans and a white, short-sleeved linen shirt, and a pair of leather sandals. Gold chain around his neck. Tasteful against his tanned skin, slightly red, perhaps, from the beach. That she had been there when that happened made her feel warm and happy.

Well aren't you just so very well-dressed? she said, straightening his collar and unbuttoning one more button so that his shirt hung open.

He smiled, almost shyly, she thought, and looked down at himself as though noticing for the first time what he had put on, and then shrugged. You look very handsome she said, running her open palm up his chest to his shoulder, and then she kissed his cheek. It was everything she could do not to kiss his neck, below his jawline, behind his ear. To run her fingers through his hair, her fingertips running up the back of his neck. To press her thinly shrouded body against him. To feel him. To feel his sturdiness. Who are you, she thought.

It was a half mile to the restaurant she'd wanted to take him to. As they turned from the side street onto one of the avenidas through the town someone going by on a quad waved to Emilia as he turned onto the side street from which they'd just come. She waved back and smiled and the man smiled and then he was out of sight. They continued walking. Past a corner shop that sold bikinis and other chic beach clothing, the two women inside lit up seeing Emilia walk by. They stopped, briefly, and exchanged hugs and kisses on the cheek, and Emilia introduced them to Damian and they smiled conspiratorial smiles to one another and to her and she said they should be going because, if they couldn't tell, Damian was terribly malnourished and likely to perish at any moment if she didn't get him a drink and some food. He good-naturedly told them that it was no rush, but she ushered him out the door the same way a child escapes a social engagement with a toy she's excited to have all to herself.

They liked you, she said as they walked away, taking his hand and walking lightly down the street beside him.

How do you know that? Did they say that in Spanish and it went entirely over my head?

No, she replied, glancing up at him slyly. I can just tell. You'd know if they didn't. As good as they may be at hiding their approval, they're absolutely shit at hiding when they do not like someone.

She glanced at him again having said this and she was pleased to see him smiling. He held her hand the rest of the way. She continued to see people she knew in many of the stores, or on the street walking or on quads or motorbikes. One old Toyota truck went by with a few leathery-looking surfers hanging out the back and they all cheered for her as they passed.

What, she asked, noticing him watching her as they walked around a corner.

Do you know everyone in this town?

She laughed then. He seemed to love to make her laugh. No, of course not.

I don't believe you, he said.

I'm sure someone's just come here who I don't know yet. Probably there are some people who I have just never met. I didn't know you before this morning, after all.

I like it, he said. She could not help but to grin.

She took a small pleasure in knowing the staff at the restaurant they went to. As if it was some joke between the two of them that they all recognized her. How familiar he felt already. She had always fallen in love easily, but this was something else. Something thrilling and dangerous.

He tried to order a beer, but she intervened in Spanish and ordered for each of them a paloma made with mezcal, with Tajin on the rim and a slice of grapefruit perched on the glass.

What did you order for me, he asked once the mesero had left.

She wouldn't say.

When the drinks came he asked if she had drugged it as well, or if she just planned to get him drunk.

I am quite confident that your size will prevent you getting drunk before me. It is I who will suffer at the hands of my own enthusiasm.

So now you're calling me fat?

No, Guapo, of course not.

He eyed her speculatively. She flickered her eyelashes at him, then reached across the table and took his hand in one of hers and he squeezed, and then took a sip from the drink. He tasted it, allowed it to swirl in his mouth, and then said: this tastes like boat fuel.

What?! she cried. Boat fuel! She threw her head back. Laughing came so easily with him. You swallowed too much ocean water I think.

No! he said, laughing along with her. Here, close your eyes and taste yours, and tell me it doesn't somehow taste vaguely like boat fuel – not the actual flavor. Just the whole sensation. Feel your drink, he said, imitating her accent.

She closed her eyes obediently and raised the glass to her lips and then he said: Wait.

He took the glass from her and he licked the Tajin from a spot on the rim.

Are you stealing my Tajin? she asked, looking very seriously offended.

Just trust me. The Tajin changes the sensation too much. It's too overpowering. Just sip from this spot, just for this. You can lick the Tajin off my tongue after if you want.

Okay, she said, I will hold you to that. Nobody steals my tajin.

Okay close your eyes like before.

She did this and raised the glass to her lips and sniffed at the drink and then took a sip and swirled it in her mouth and swallowed and she thought somehow that he had been right. That this drink she'd always taken at every opportunity was now transformed and would forever, in spite of her own desires or preferences, taste of boat fuel. It wasn't a bad flavor, as he'd said. Not even a bad association, somehow. Something about the musk of the mezcal and the sour astringent of the grapefruit. It all came together, and she had to admit that he was right.

You're right, she said, opening her eyes.

What was that? he asked teasingly, leaning forward as if to hear her better. He cupped one hand behind his ear. She leaned across the table and grabbed the unbuttoned portion of his shirt in her fist and pulled him forward somehow carefully, and then said very close to his face, their noses touching, their eyes on one another's: Yes, you were right. Now I'm taking my Tajin back. And then she kissed him, her tongue darting into his mouth, warm, and still actually tasting slightly of Tajin, and then she released him. She sat back, and dabbed at the corner of her mouth with her napkin.

Where did you come from? he asked her after a moment. He had leaned back in his chair comfortably.

Your wildest dreams.

Nonsense.

What, you don't have dreams?

He did not smile. I have dreams – but none of them come even remotely close to you. He took a sip, and put the glass back down.

She tucked a strand of hair behind her ear and smiled privately to herself.

She ordered the food for both of them, everything to share, and many of the things she fed a first bite to him, or he to her, and they agreed on everything except the shrimp tacos. He insisted that the camarones on the beach were better. She insisted on teaching him to pronounce it correctly. When he had done it to her satisfaction, she toasted his quickly improving Spanish. In no time, you'll be able to move here and see me whenever you want, she said. As the words came out of her mouth she knew how reckless they had been, but it was too late to take them back and she wouldn't have done it even if she could. In response to this comment, he said simply: Don't tease me.

After dinner they walked down the beach for the equivalent of two or three blocks between beach access points, and the sun set in this time, as though they had planned it perfectly, even though they hadn't. Emilia took note of this fact and considered it a good omen that things seemed to be falling so perfectly into place for them on this night. The sunset itself was richer in the colors of the ocean than the colors in the sky, but still it captivated them both, and for a while, they stood there on the beach, she holding her shoes, he holding his, his jeans cuffed at the bottom, their bare feet in the sand, his arm around her waist, resting comfortably on her hip, her head inclined and resting on the inside of his shoulder. The breeze off the ocean cooled their skin pleasantly. This really is a beautiful place, he said, and she agreed, adding that it seemed to have some sort of magic to it. It's something, he replied. She looked up at him once or twice, and for a brief moment that she hoped desperately to remember, she watched him watching the ocean.

I've seen this ocean several times since I got here. Earlier today, obviously, but also before we left the beach this afternoon, and now, and once yesterday when I first arrived. It's been a different color every time.

She is very much alive, Emilia answered, smiling, an affectionate inflection in her voice.

For a while they were quiet. The dusk grew, and the beach cleared as the sunset walkers departed. The sounds of flamenco music arrived, watery, from down the beach. Besides that and the occasional addition of half-heard conversations, the predominant soundtrack was the ocean waves and their ceaseless breaking, a kind of soft, rolling white noise, and the sound of the night breeze in the palms.

I don't remember the last time I've felt this relaxed, Damian said after a while.

She looked up at him then, he still looking out at the water, and she turned into him and wrapped her arms around his waist, and let her head rest on his chest. He threaded his fingers through her hair and held her there, and in this way they stayed for what felt like a generously lingering while, until she, sensing the energy rising again between them, suggested they go for a drink. He looked down into her open, happy face, and nodded, and then he kissed her forehead and she nearly purred.

La Noche

They arrived at a tequila bar on the Avenida Revolución, a place decorated mostly in white, with full-length glass windows that looked out on the cobblestone street and the shuttered tiendas and the new twilight. They chose a small table in the back corner, the stone walls cool even after a day of torrential sun which had baked most of the town warm until long after dark. They sat side by side on a cushioned booth that had been built into the wall, with several throw pillows positioned such that it felt very natural to sit touching one another. He had picked that table, which she noticed, and liked. She allowed him to order his own drink – a phrase she used in her mind, hilarious almost to her, since he was so very clearly in control of everything even though this was her town. He ordered a mezcal flight, and she prodded him that she had apparently made an impression with the boat fuel. When in Mexico, you know, he replied. Then he had touched her thigh, large warm palm on the smooth, soft skin of her leg.

The drinks went down quickly and they ordered another round, each of them ordering palomas this time. As they drank and talked he kept his hand almost constantly on her leg, as though he was making sure to keep her near him. She felt small in his grasp, and excitingly vulnerable. She occasionally would look down and see his hand on her bare thigh, so sturdy, the hairs on the back of his hand catching the gentle light from the bar, the veins sticking out from his knuckles all the way to where his arm disappeared beneath his shirt sleeve. He would look so good in a wedding ring. The thought shocked her and she pushed it from her mind, mostly because she wasn't sure she even believed in marriage – had, in fact, intently not believed in marriage for her entire adult life. Commitment in general was something that almost made her skin crawl. Commitment was for the weak. It was for those who couldn't trust in the way things are. It was a crutch. People change too often for life-long promises. She looked at his hand there on her leg again and she wanted it to belong to her. She could not understand what was happening. She could force herself to focus on his eyes. But then she would look at his lips.

She looked out at the avenida and nodded absently to something he was saying. Something about hydroelectric power and how disruptive it actually was to places exactly like this – maybe not this town specifically – but how Mexico as a country had suffered greatly from the mismanagement of water rights in the United States. The street moved with people on foot, on motorbikes, the occasional car – too big seeming, the cars – or a truck, and many, many golfcarts. A mix of nationalities. Who even considers water rights, she wondered. How conscientious of him. She let her fingers play passively with the collar of his shirt, with the fringe of hair at the back of his neck.

You're not listening to anything I'm saying, are you, he asked, smiling.

She looked back at him, drawn back to presence, called out. She almost wanted to blush – who thinks about wanting to blush, she wondered – but she saw his smiling eyes, his mouth easily half-open, waiting for her response. He waited for her. Miles ahead and he waited for her. She looked from his eyes to his mouth. I was listening, she half-lied. She ran her hand down his arm. I think I'm feeling a little drunk. She flickered her eyelashes at him but realized even in the moment of doing it that it hadn't been intentional.

He laughed easily, some new ease in his demeanor, and she realized he was possibly a little drunk, too. Not a lot. Not beyond control. Just loosened. She wanted to dance with him. She motioned to the bartender to bring the cuenta and he physically stopped her reaching for her purse when she went to pay and she nearly gasped, moved inside by his simple act of grabbing her wrist. The way he smiled as he told her with his body exactly what to do, and what not to do. And then sliding a fold of pesos into the crystal tumbler in which the check had arrived, he paused, looking at it, then he looked at her.

It's customary to tip here, right? he asked her. He was so sincere, she almost kissed him again. Yes, she said. She was aware of blinking more times than was necessary. As though the intensity of his gaze compelled her to blink more frequently. And it's the quickest way to make friends, she added, especially as a tourista. She rose to standing and bent and kissed his cheek as she said the last part, and lingered for a moment, smelling him. She bent at the waist to kiss him, and he saw the way her body moved in the dress she wore. Saw the skirt rise up the backs of her thighs in the obscure, lighted reflection of her in the windowglass. He wanted to trace the lines of her tattoos. Come, she said, let's go dance.

Dance? he said, surprised. No, I don't dance. I am absolutely no good at dancing.

Absolutely no good at dancing, she mocked, mimicking his accent. Come on. She took his hand and he allowed her to help him stand. Where are we going? he asked.

On the street, she pressed herself shamelessly against him, grabbing the sides of his shirt in her hands, and kissed his neck. Follow me, she said.

She danced down the street leading him by the hand, having waved without looking to the bartender, whom of course she knew, and he watched the low hem of her dress as she went before him and he watched the way her hair bounced and felt the cool of the humid night and smelled the sea, though still faintly, subtly, the way he had before, and he drew it deeply into his nose and exhaled more air than he had taken in over the last five years. He was sure there had been people she knew when they left, and she kissed him like that in front of them. There was a lot to that, he thought. Or hoped.

He wondered where she was taking him but if he was honest with himself he didn't care, and it wasn't just that he'd had a few drinks, and it wasn't just that he was on vacation. It was, he realized, that he trusted her, which he thought was honestly kind of insane, because she was absolutely the most free-spirited, wild person he'd ever met, much less fallen in love with. And then it hit him. He was falling in love with her. This thought made him smile, because he was fairly certain she was falling in love with him too, though he'd never been a good judge of that, if he was honest with himself. The air was cool on his skin and her hand was cool and electric and alive and he watched her and he tried not to stumble on the uneven streets and sidewalks as they passed the closed-up businesses and the restaurants that had been open when they'd passed before but were now shut down. They went down the Calle Marlin to the beach access and then across the sand, she still leading him by the hand and he going wherever she wanted to take him, to a group of people in front of a DJ booth that looked out on the beach. There were maybe fifty people gathered around, most of them dancing, some sitting or lounging around small fires that had been built in sandy fire pits at the center of circular wooden benches fitted with cushions. The ocean folded over itself beyond in the dark and he could hear it and smell it and nearly taste the salt it left on his lips in the humid mist that seemed to hang over everything. The song that had been playing when they arrived ended, or rather melted into the next song, and she took his hand and twirled herself and then brought herself close to him, her body pressing against his, her hips moving to the music, her eyes closed, her hands finding purchase on different parts of his chest, or his waist, or his neck. Or caressing her own body as she pressed into him – this he found most erotic – and always he was aware of her, of her body, of her position relative to him, of her movements and the way they interacted with him. As though he questioned whether she wanted him. It was obvious, he knew. Had been all day. She'd talked to him on the beach. She had leaned into him in the waves. Still he questioned, the same way someone would question the reality of winning the lottery even if the winning ticket was in-hand and the numbers on the board and the confetti falling. He watched her in the strobing lights and he could no longer focus his eyes and his thoughts melted away. She moved once again toward him and he touched her hips, or felt the smooth skin of her legs, the hem of her dress yielding to his fingertips. He could not help but move with her. It was like they were already making love, and he found himself almost painfully turned on. His thoughts receded. He no longer had them. They had left him. It was all feeling. This was new territory.

They were not long on the beach, and they were not long walking back to her house, stopping at least once every hundred feet or so to kiss and to touch each other and to laugh at the freedom that had suddenly inhabited them both. They were quick with the door, and their lips had not separated as they unlocked the latch, nor as she unbuttoned his shirt nor as he hoisted her against the wall, her dress climbing her thighs and his hands holding her firmly as he kissed her and her arms wrapped his neck and her legs parted around him.

They no longer spoke. Only made their animal noises in the dark as the sounds of the waves came in through the window and the wind moved the curtains and they each felt the pressure of the other's skin. They moved like water around the room. He holding her. The two of them pressing against each other and crashing into walls, into furniture, her dress thrown on a chair, she dancing backwards before him, twisting her hips sensually, wanting, needing, falling together onto the bed. He growled at her – it was all he could do. Fuck, I want you, he thought, maybe, if his thoughts had words. When he grabbed her it was his skin on hers and when he kissed her everywhere from the arch of her foot to the back of her knee and to the inside of her thigh and up her stomach and across her ribs curved in the moonlight through the window, and her breasts and up and back down her collar bone – when he kissed each of the fingers on her right hand, and when he kissed her forehead, and her ear, and the tip of her nose, which made her laugh with joy, and then her cheek, and the concave arc beneath her chin which made her gasp and arch her back, and finally, desperately almost her mouth – and when he entered her it was slowly and their eyes were locked and he watched as he pushed her further from reason and further from reality and she watched as his eyes rolled involuntarily at the all-consuming presence of her body around him. Their foreheads met, a grasping at the tangible world, some energetic need for knowing that they were there together. I am here, he said to her. And I am also, she said in return. Not with words. With contact.

At first what she'd felt was the intensity of his presence. The commitment he exuded, to the moment, to her, to himself. This was a conscious choice, she knew. He'd shown that with every time he could've had her and had chosen not to take her. This, is what I want, he said with his body. But she felt him hold back, too. To be polite. Out of respect, for her, for her body, for the rules he still believed. And then she kissed up his neck, and she bit his ear, hard.

In the heat of instinct he grabbed her throat. Pressed her to the bed. He looked at her, a flame in his eyes, his hand around her neck, and she looked back at him with an even greater intensity. Like an invitation. A challenge. Take me. There was some silent ancient conversation between their eyes in that moment. Some grand understanding, the complexity of respect and degradation played out in sexual theater in the course of an instant. And he, seeing the excitement in her eyes, slapped her, though he didn't know why. A flicker of temporary awareness. A question. Is that okay? Yes, I like it. Give it to me. Harder. Fuck me. I need you.

He grabbed a fistful of her hair and turned her on her stomach, and she arched desperately toward him, grabbing handfulls of sheets with both hands, begging him with every physical insinuation available to her to take her completely. And he did. He pressed into her so deeply she felt herself coming apart. It was nearly more than she could handle but he whispered in her ear in that exact moment that she felt so incredible and she felt the heat and the intensity of his arousal and it softened her to him, made it such that she would've died in his hands if it was what he'd wanted. Take me, she breathed. Fuck me, please. Yes – it was a plea. It was all she'd ever needed. The way the ocean pulled her out, pushed her in, pushed her down. The way a storm tore from her the decision to live or to die. It was the power of the wave. He was in that moment the earth and she was the moon and even as she lent the force of her gravity unto him he still moved of his own accord and she followed. She drew out the best in him, but she followed him, always. And then he was coming, and she felt him deep inside of her and she felt herself contract against him, and in this way they died together, just for a moment, the same way a person dies beneath the water when there are forces at play beyond the scope of human comprehension.

Fuck, I'm sorry, he said. He panted against her neck, his chest against her back, the two of them flat on the bed, except for her hips which she still reached animalistically toward him. She laughed, but she could not speak. Choking on him still, and his hands weren't even around her neck. He kissed her temples and his hand found the small of her waist and he gripped her, he still inside her, and he exhaled heavily behind her, and then he collapsed on top of her.

His weight was immense. It was more than the sum of his physical mass. You're an animal, she said to him, feeling him crush her, pleasantly suffocated almost. I've never done that before, he said. I don't even know where that came from.

It was in you, she said. I just brought it out.

If you say so, he said. It was okay? I didn't hurt you?

No, she said lightly, pleasantly exhausted. I loved it. It was perfect.

Okay, he said. He shifted his weight, feeling that he should make some space for her beneath him. He didn't roll off. Just shifted such that his weight went into his arms and his legs more and less completely on her body, which felt so small beneath him. He breathed deeply the smell of her, the smell of the two of them, still inside her, still enveloped by her warmth, and she enveloped by his entire body. That's what it is, she thought. We are inside each other. Like breathing each other in, no barriers between us. How luxurious. He had surrendered to the effect she'd had upon him, and it was in this moment that he said that he loved her.

She laughed aloud. Shhh, she said, smiling happily. Don't speak. But he had said it, and meant it. And she had liked it for a fraction of an instant, at least. I'm sorry, he said then. I just...

Shhh, she said again, gently, softly, soothingly. She ran her fingers up through his hair, reaching behind her, pulling him to herself even as he was atop of her and she was face-down on the bed. She rolled over, he slipping out of her, she feeling him leak out of her onto the bed. They were on one side of the bed, could sleep on the other. It's okay, she said. Come here. She held him. He moved down that his head could rest on her chest and she could hold him. His arms wrapped her waist. The narrow part of her waist. The part a corset would have suffocated. And yet his arms were not suffocating. They kept space for her to breathe. Hadn't he done that always. All day, she thought, and laughed. Always, today. What was the difference. He held her and let her breathe. Eagles diving together, so much air for both of them, wings strong and capable, the wind rushing past, and freedom. And wasn't that what she'd always wanted? To be held and free at the same time. She exhaled heavily, ran her fingers through his hair. He felt the fall of her chest. He sank into her. He fell asleep instantly in the space made by her surrender. And she did too.

El Amanecer

He heard the roosters first, and wondered in the darkness at the hour. He looked sideways amidst the dull pressure in his head and found her sleeping, facing him, sprawled endearingly. Even in sleep she was chaotic and what did he find to love in that? Only everything. As he watched her sleep, he himself only half-awake, he had the feeling of something beginning. He slipped back into a dream shortly after. A dream of water. Of waves. Of sun. No land in sight, just the ocean for miles in all directions and no fear, either. Just the ocean. Just the ocean.

When he woke as the sun came finally through the windows it was not the light that had actually woken him but her body coming alongside his, her back pressed to him, she on her side and facing away, but searching for him. He turned, tucked his arm beneath his head. His top arm wrapped her and she laced her fingers into his and pressed further against him. She was perhaps still asleep. He, too. Who could say in that early dim light. She pressed her naked body against him again in that way that suggested that she felt they could not – would never – get close enough to satisfy her need to touch him. He became hard, and she pressed against him again. Small, sleepy movements, both of them, and a burning, some warm thing alive between them. She reached behind and slid him inside her, the two of them still for a moment in their union. And then the slow, half-sleep lovemaking and their bodies rocking eternally in the space between the dark of night and the brilliance of morning. They fell back asleep in exactly this position and he did not wake again until it was mid-morning. She had been awake for some time when he opened his eyes and it was under her gaze that he resumed consciousness. She was lying there, her head propped in her hand, her hair half-covering her face, her body uncovered and the room warm and still. When he saw her he smiled, and she smiled, too. A moment suspended. How many still moments make up a life, he wondered. She found it endearing and magical the way love could actually stop time. Was this? she thought. Was this love. Oh who cares what it's called. He watched her, and she allowed herself to be watched. Did you sleep? she asked.

He nodded, but did not speak. Good, she said. She kissed him and then she got out of bed.

It was too soon, her departure. He would've liked for her to climb on top of him. To maybe take him in her mouth. Or just to lay on his chest for a while. Already, every moment without touching her was an ache. Jesus Christ, he thought. What are you doing to yourself.

She had pulled on a pair of shorts that hardly covered anything and she was piling her hair on top of her head standing by the bed, facing away. He watched her passively. She looked over her shoulder and asked what he was looking at. You, he said. Good, she replied. That's what I was hoping. Are you hungry? Would you like some breakfast? Coffee? Tea?

You're a morning person, aren't you, he said.

Of course! she said. And a night person. I'm an any-time-of-day person. Don't you like the mornings?

He kind of grunted and burrowed into the pillow. She laughed and he had to conceal his smile. Fuck, he thought. I'm really done for.

She made a pot of coffee and brought some over to him in bed, and he sat up and held the steaming mug in both of his hands.

Look at the way the light catches the steam, she said, sitting on the bed beside him. Isn't it so beautiful?

You're so beautiful, he said, and took a sip, which was still too hot and he knew it would be but he needed to do something with his mouth before he said anything else. Burn the stupidity from his tongue, maybe. She kissed his shoulder.

I have a yoga class in half an hour, she said. You're welcome to stay here if you like. I'll be back after the class. Maybe we could walk to the beach for a swim?

He looked from the black, mirrory surface of the coffee to her face, so bright, so happy. I'd like that, he said. Good, she replied. That's what I wanted you to say.

Hey, about last night. We didn't use protection and I—

It's okay, she said smiling and putting her hand, still warm from the mug, on his forearm. I take birth control. It's no problem, really. I would've stopped you, it's my responsibility, too, you know.

No, it's not really – I should've used a condom.

Shh, she said. It's okay, Damian. I loved it. I loved all of it. It was perfect.

She looked in his eyes as she said this and her expression was so earnest and so kind and so forgiving. Okay, he replied. I'm still sorry.

Don't be, she said again. I'm not sorry.

Okay, then I'm not sorry either.

Good.

Also, about what I said at the end...

What, that you love me?

Yes, that, he said, looking up at the ceiling and smiling in spite of himself, sighing in surrender to the acknowledgement of his own blunder.

Well, did you mean it?

Obviously yes I did. Do. Still, I probably should've had more restra—

No, if you meant it, you were right to say it. Her resolution in this statement was absolute.

But it made you feel uncomfortable, didn't it?

Me? No – surprised, maybe. I didn't expect it, but not uncomfortable.

He nodded.

I think we are sometimes too careful with our words, when the whole point of them is to express what's alive within us, to share it with the world, or with those we love.

Words can hurt people, though. Badly, sometimes.

Well, yes of course. That's not what I mean. Maybe I'm explaining myself poorly. I just mean, especially when it comes to telling people compliments or showing our love or being honest about something we're feeling, I think those are things that need to be shared. For example, I can tell you that last night at the bar I thought that your hand would look very good in a wedding ring. I wanted it to be the hand of the man who belonged to me. I've never really wanted that before, not as an adult at least. I've always been very against marriage or any sort of life-long commitment because who even knows what they will want in two years or twenty. But I felt it last night. Who knows what it means. Probably it doesn't mean anything – just that I felt it.

He was watching the steam rising from his mug and listening to her words and inside of him was a warmth that he had never felt, at least consciously. Maybe as a child. Maybe not even then, though.

But that's the other thing, isn't it, she went on. We should speak freely, I think, but also allow each other to say what we feel in the moment and not hold each other to it too seriously. Like, you love me now, loved me last night. Maybe I love you too. But it will change. That was then, this is now, and what will come will come, because of course things would change, wouldn't they? Of course they would, and when they change we have to be free to speak life to the change, too. It should not be so bad to say you love someone, or that you've thought of marrying them, and then to still allow yourself space to realize that perhaps it was a fleeting intensity that needed to be spoken.

He was frowning now, not necessarily in disagreement, but in thought, maybe even in dialog with himself somehow about what she was saying. I don't know about that part, he said. I feel like our word is one of the things we have to give each other that means something. If you can't trust someone's word, how can you trust them? It would make their words so meaningless.

I disagree – I would say that if someone can't be honest about the changes in their heart, how can you trust them?

He thought about this. It had to be both, he thought. To be honest, and to be careful with one's words. I think, he said after a moment, that it's important, obviously, to speak the truth of what you're feeling. I guess I just think it's a person's responsibility to not speak every fleeting impulse, which obviously I didn't do a very good job of last night.

It's okay, she said. I am very sexy and you were lost in me. She said this as though it were an irrefutable truth.

He laughed then, endeared brilliantly by her easy humor even amidst a serious conversation – a disagreement at that. Yes, okay, I'll give myself a pass on that one. How can she be so confident, he thought. And for her part, she was aware of being very arrogant in that moment but it was all part of the game. Why not? It was very fun.

I see what you're saying though, she said after a moment. I do. And to that point, I think that sometimes what we believe is careful examination of what we say, before we say it – sometimes we're just trying to polish something difficult to say. You know? Is that the right phrase? Like almost a form of manipulation. Choosing words too carefully feels almost deceitful, doesn't it?

I don't think it does. But I see what you mean, too. Of course some people manipulate their manner of saying something in order to make it sound a certain way. Lying by omission, for example.

Yes, exactly. That is exactly what I mean. She threw her hands in the air in agreement. Her face was so wide and happy. And other things, she said, but that's a very good example. She looked at the clock on the microwave and stood up. I have to get ready to go, she said. But I look forward to continuing this conversation later. She ran her hand down the back of his head and across his shoulder and then walked into the bathroom.

He sat back against the headboard, the mug of coffee now empty, held loosely in his hands, and closed his eyes. He could hear the sounds of the town, the big water trucks that rumbled loudly through the city, much too large for the streets, but accommodated with a sort of friendly tolerance and mutual respect. He heard the roosters call incessantly from all parts of the town, confused, he thought, because it was already morning. He would come to know they crowed regardless of the time of day or night and that nobody really paid them any mind. He heard the little parrots in the trees outside chattering away, the voices of people passing and speaking to each other in Spanish and he picked out a few words here and there, but mostly did not understand anything. He heard the sound of the sink in her bathroom running intermittently, small bursts, and the sounds of the bathroom cabinet door opening and closing, products set on the concrete countertop. He swore he could hear the sunshine, too. And the ocean, even though it was too far to be really heard during the daytime. Heard it all maybe, the entire world in some vague and resonant song on the wind. He drew a breath. She flicked off the bathroom light. You will be here when I get back? she asked. He opened his eyes, looked at her, nodded, smiled. Unless they come for me, he said.

She kissed his forehead. I hope they wait until I get back so I can kiss you again once more before they take you.

I will ask them to delay their taking of me, he said. For you. Enjoy your class.

She smiled, her lips against his. Mi amor, she said. Thank you, enjoy the morning.

I love you, he said. She touched his cheek and smiled at him. Beware, she said, the fine line between love and possession. And only speak it when it is love.

Where did you even come from, he asked her.

Your wildest dreams, she said. I've come to rescue you.

Or wreck me.

Well, one or the other, she said. And then she was gone.

El Día

After she'd left he set his mug on the bedside table and slid down into the bed again, pushing the covers down to his waist, interlacing his fingers under the pillow beneath his head. The ceiling fan moved the air over his bare skin and he silently thanked whoever had invented ceiling fans. He thought maybe he would sleep but instead stared at the ceiling beams and the concave bricks that arced between them, at the burnmarks from their firing, at the cream-colored mortar between them, at the shadows from the sun that filtered through the curtains.

And she had walked out the door, her yoga mat slung over her shoulder with its woven strap, a gift from a friend at her last birthday, and she'd swung her leg over the motorbike and pulled the clutch and pressed the starter with her thumb and felt it sputter momentarily and then the soft purr of it between her legs. She turned the bike around and began down the street. She loved the feel of the wind in her hair and she loved the way the cobblestone streets made the bike vibrate as she rode. The sun was bright and hot and the day was interminably humid and she felt the sweat on her brow even as she rode, but she did not resent the heat. Savor the wind all the more, she thought. Blessed wind. Blessed sun.

From the bed he let his mind wander in a sort of placid meander through the recollection of what had happened over the last twenty-four hours and what was to come in the following forty-eight. He had fallen in love. Is that the right word for it, he wondered. Or the right phrase. It was illogically fast, but her pull was illogically strong. Besides, this was what you did – maybe not on vacation in a foreign country and maybe not in the span of a day, but to fall in love was one of life's benchmarks, and then you would get married and have children, or not, but in any case the love had to be there at some point, and who was he to decide how such things were delivered. He rubbed his eyes and wondered if there was more coffee.

She rode through the town toward the big hill off of Avenida Revolución and she felt the mist off the bike's front tire from the wet streets that had in some places just been washed, and she saw the tiendas opening and some of the restaurantes open with their chairs and tables set out in the street. The people she knew waved at her and she smiled and waved back. She passed again the tienda de ropa that her friends owned and saw Maria just arriving and pulling up the metal safety doors and she waved and continued on. The sun was bright and clear and the sky free, entirely, of clouds. The town had a fresh smell, the wind generously out of the west on this day instead of the south, and it was blowing in the scent of the ocean. She came upon a car stopped in the road, its flashers on, back hatch open, and someone unloading something in boxes into a closed quiosco and she navigated around it, slipping between an oncoming motorbike and the stopped car and then another pedestrian, and she felt the throb of competence like a proud piece in her chest.

There was more coffee, and he poured it into his cup, though it was no longer steaming. He thought of microwaving it, but decided to drink it only warm. He looked at the bed but felt like it was time to move his legs a bit. So he walked around the small house and almost absently looked at her things. There were little treasures everywhere. Small clay figures, shells, crystals, a tarot deck, an incense burner with ashes in small cylindrical clumps beneath the stick that stood half-burned in the holder. He looked without seeing at the books on her shelf, most of them in Spanish, but some in English. A couple, actually, in French. Can she speak French, he wondered. And what now? his thoughts continued. What now old boy. You fly home in two days. Tomorrow night, actually. And then what? She's not leaving. She was made for this place, or it for her. Or whatever – she's not going anywhere. And you wouldn't ask her to anyway. What, trade this for a craftsman style house on a dirt road in the forest in Idaho? Well, we have hot springs, he imagined himself telling her, half in jest. No, she's not moving. And you? What, you're going to cancel your flight. Or better yet, just miss it. That would be hilariously carefree of you, wouldn't it? He almost laughed aloud at this thought. Just don't show up, he told himself. Yeah, that's it.

Up and over the big hill past the construction of the new apartamentos, the obreros hand-mixing concrete and hammering nails from their well-used wooden forms, fashioned again and again into the molds for more houses than anyone could count. The boards themselves employed in the construction of homes, like the obreros, nameless to the final inhabitants, invaluable to the world. They were gone in a flash as she turned her attention to the speed bumps and shot the narrow gap in the bumps down the middle of the street, cutting right again to allow space for a golfcart to pass her going the opposite direction. The little girl in the cart beside her mother looked at her and smiled and actually waved, and Emilia grinned back and winked and then they were gone, too. She descended the other side of the hill and turned onto Punta de Mita and shortly thereafter parked the bike in the shade of the big tree in front of the studio. Kickstand down, the bike warm beneath her bare legs, she swung her leg over as Aditi called out from the doorway in welcome.

He pulled a record from a milk crate, Jackson Browne Remastered, and put it on the turntable. Then he picked it up again, blew some dust from the top, and put it back down. He thought about getting on the plane, about getting on the plane alone. You're never going to forget her, he thought. She will literally haunt you forever. So what, stay. Miss the flight, or cancel it if it helps you sleep better. Better yet, just reschedule. Stay a few more days. Stay a week. Call into work and say you got dysentery. Or giardia. Whatever you can catch down here. Don't think about that, you'll actually get sick. He'd started side two of the record without really meaning to and as he swam in this sea of thoughts about what in the world he was going to do, the bridge refrain came through and the harmonies actually made him pause. Something about the music and the light and the smell of the coffee. The sheets on the bed, the indent of her body still somehow where she had slept, her shape still on her pillow. He could still see her there in the partial dark of early morning, the way her hair covered her face and even still he could tell she was smiling. Who smiles in their sleep. Maybe you'd be happier here he thought. More peace in this little serving than you've ever known in your entire life.

She bounced up to Aditi and gave her a hug, grinning widely. Someone's happy today, she said. Not just happy, you're glowing! You look like you've been properly fucked.

Aditi! she said, feigning offence. Don't talk about it that way!

Well, what am I supposed to say?

I don't know, something a little... sweeter?

But you did, didn't you...

She looked away, at the bright street, at the cars and trucks going by, smiling to herself. When she looked back to the woman in the door she had lights in her eyes. She nodded.

Ooh, goodie – well bring all that lovely ephemeral, buoyant energy to class. You'll need a strap and two blocks unless you're feeling extra flexible today.

You're too much, Emilia said, pressing her shoulder as she passed.

He looked through his archived emails on his phone and found his flight confirmation, and then scrolled down to the bottom to where the phone number was listed for customer service. He taped the number and the window appeared to initiate the call. He pressed the side button on the phone and the screen went dark. She probably doesn't even want you to stay, he thought. Yes, but then why did she ask me to stay at her place while she was gone. Who trusts a stranger like that in their home alone. She probably does this a lot, actually. She probably feasts on tourists. The thought made him chuckle. Like she was some small, gorgeous, sexually deviant carnivore satiating her need for animalistic sex with men from the Potato State she'd picked up on the beach. The affection he felt for her chaos was actually invigorating. He wanted her again. He wondered how long it would be before she returned. He ran the timeline of an average hour-long class, when she'd left, how long it must take her to get there, and back. Wondered, also, if she'd stop anywhere. Maybe she wanted him to actually leave while she was away. That would be a very clean and dignified way to do it. Give him the open door, but the option to stay. Stay out longer than necessary, each of them having expressed their positive intent, and each of them walking away silently, leaving everyone's dignity intact. But didn't she just this morning tout the importance of honest words? She wouldn't have manipulated the situation like that. He took a drink of the coffee and realized it was better now that it wasn't so hot. He could actually taste it, even in spite of the burn on the tip of his tongue from before. Or maybe she had burned him when he kissed her. Devil woman. He smiled.

The class was hard, and she sweated profusely, using a towel here and there to wipe the puddles from her mat that she not slip on them in the challenging balance poses. She relished the challenge, the push within her to hold for one more breath, one more breath, always one more breath. And then the sweet release. She loved how it felt to feel strong. To feel capable. There it was again, to feel capable. And then she thought of him, and the way she loved to be directed by him. Not because he thought she couldn't – or that he needed the control. It was just assumed in the chemistry between them that he was in charge and she would happily follow him. I'm like a helpless little puppy when he is around, she thought. Uttana Shishosana – puppy pose, Aditi called out. Get out of my head, Emilia thought, smiling. And why do you have to use the Sanskrit words too. It had always bothered her. Some sort of yoga teacher superiority. What a silly thing to worry about, she thought. But it wasn't really worry. It was like the thought of the worry – as though it were some part of a different version of herself and that in this headspace, in this way of being on this particular day it did not really bother her at all. Like she could watch it and laugh kindly at the frivolousness of everything except for love.

When she came home he was sitting in a chair by the kitchen window, reading a book she recognized as one of her own. It was The Alchemist. An illustrated version, with paintings by the French artist Moebius. She loved that book, and she loved that he had found it and chosen it. He looked up at the sound of the door and seeing her, smiled, and then rose to help her with the things she carried.

Hello handsome, she said, standing on tiptoes to kiss his cheek. Are you hungry?

Not ravenous, he said.

Mmm, she said happily. I like that word. Well I stopped by the French bakery and picked up some bread things for us in case you were hungry. Smell, she directed, and opened the brown paper bag holding it up enough for the scent to escape toward him. He bent, sniffed, and then said: Okay, now I'm hungry. Good, she said. Now we have reached the correct answer. She handed him the bag and asked if he would slice the bread.

You seem to have a knack for reading all my favorite books, she said from the other room as she propped her yoga mat in the corner.

Do I? he asked from the kitchen. He was slicing the baguette and some cheese she had told him to get from the fridge, and putting little assemblies of the two on a plate. She returned and put her hand on his lower back, still bare, though he had at some point put on his jeans. She leaned into his shoulder with her lips. She smelled him. You smell good, she said.

He looked at her. What do I smell like?

Mmm, like you. Nothing I could name. Maybe just the slightest bit like me. It's just a good smell.

I was worried I would smell bad since I haven't showered this morning.

She shook her head, her lips still against his skin.

I assume these are meant to go together, he said, pointing with the knife at the cheese and the bread he was slicing. She nodded, still without removing her lips from his shoulder. Oh, she said suddenly. This, too. She fetched a large tomato and set it down beside the cutting board. I'm going to change, she added. I'm horribly sweaty.

Need any help, he asked over his shoulder. He did not expect a response, much less a favorable one. In fact as soon as he'd said it he had regretted it.

If you want, she said insinuatingly. He looked over his shoulder again in time to see her disappear around the corner into her room as she was pulling her top off over her head. He paused, set the knife down, and followed her.

When he turned the corner into her room she was waiting for him, still in her shorts, and when he came in she jumped on him and immediately started kissing him. You are ruining me for anyone else, he said through her kisses. She placed her index finger against his lips and said shhh. Oh you shhh, he said. He laid her down on the bed and slid her shorts over her hips and then he kissed down the center of her stomach so slowly it made her ache inside. When he kissed between her legs she was already very wet, and she felt the muscle of his tongue contact her most sensitive parts with almost overwhelming sensation. He had his hands on the outside of her thighs, high up where they met her hips, and he was holding her down on the bed and in his hands there was the sentiment that she wasn't going anywhere until he had reduced her to nothing but feeling and maybe some dying yelp to God. She was very close already to that nirvanic end and she ran her fingers through his hair as he did things with his mouth that she had never experienced. She cried out, gasping, into the still midmorning air. He moaned into her as he felt her come, and then he kissed the insides of her thighs and the low bowl of her stomach beneath her navel and he bit softly the skin taught upon the rise of her pelvis and he ran one hand over her breast and then as though he were not some full-grown man she pulled him up and over her like a blanket and he lay once again on her chest and she stroked the shadow of stubble on his jaw and she ran her delicate little fingers behind his ear and she pulled on his earlobe and she smoothed back his eyebrows and she kissed the top of his head and then exhaled a thousand years of loneliness.

What the hell, she said, was that. She felt him smile against her. Happy girl? he asked. Very happy girl, she replied. Good. He kissed her sternum and then relaxed back into her arms. How did you learn to do this?

I didn't really learn, so to speak.

Well you clearly know what you're doing.

Hmm, he said after a moment. I'm just doing what feels right. I actually haven't really been with very many people.

How many?

You can't ask that! he said, looking up at her.

I just did. I've been with twenty-five men.

He looked at her, and then kissed the center of her chest.

And seventeen women, she added.

He laughed and it was the sort of laugh where even he was not sure if she was joking or being very serious and that in any case he didn't really care. What would you expect with a woman that beautiful. The number was actually lower than he would've thought, but he didn't say this.

And you, she asked into his hair, as if asking it directly of his head.

Far fewer, he replied.

How many? I'm not your first, certainly.

Ha, no, he said. You're not my first. What, did you think I was a virgin or something. No, you're not my first.

Ten, then, she said.

Fewer, he replied.

Five?

He shook his head against her chest where she held him.

Well tell me, then.

He looked at her, looked into her eyes, smiled. She was so good.

You're my fourth, he said. That's probably embarrassing, isn't it.

Seriously? she asked. He could feel that she had lifted her head to look at him.

Really really.

I think that's actually very admirable, she said after a moment, resting her head back down on the bed. And to be honest it makes me feel very special.

What are we doing, he asked then.

Right now we are lying together, and then we will eat, and then we will go for a walk. She was making small soft drawings with her fingernails on his back.

And after that?

Who knows? Maybe swim? Or eat something for dinner. Maybe you will make love to me again.

And tomorrow, and the next day?

She laughed easily. Who knows what tomorrow will hold anyway. Are you worried about it? We have right now, after all. The most important moment of all.

He nodded and did not ask anything else, and she could feel something in him withdraw.

I might hope that every day could be this wonderful, though. And having said this she closed her eyes and she could feel something rise again within him, and in that moment she wondered if the moon was ever scared of the power she held over the sea.

La Tormenta

In the heat of high noon they walked together again through the town to his place and then to a quiosco for a bottle of wine and then on to the beach. They took a path she wanted to show him that went through the jungle instead of along the road with all the resorts and touristy restaurants. The path wound steeply up and when she looked back at him on the steps expecting to see him a ways behind and struggling to keep up, he was right behind her and it didn't even look as if he was breathing hard.

Mister fit, she teased. It's the altitude, he said. Where I live is more than 6,000 feet above sea level. That's what, almost 2,000 meters? The air here makes it easy for me. Ah, sure, sure, she said, she herself out of breath. It's okay – here I am thinking I've got you beat with this little walk and you aren't even working hard. In this moment, thrilled by her strength, by the challenge of the hill, she thrilled also at the fact of his strength having outdone her own. Are you looking at my butt while we walk?

I'm not an animal, he replied.

She looked back over her shoulder, mischievously. Sure you are, I've seen it. A mere man does not make love like that.

He laughed jovially. You do something to me, he said.

And then she stopped and turned around to face him. Are you having a good time? she asked with incredible sincerity.

Of course, he said. Why?

Because there's sadness in your eyes.

He paused, looking out at the view. They could see the ocean from this vantage point and he watched the waves break over the rocks at the base of the hill and he watched farther up how the tiny specks of people rose and fell with the ocean's perpetual undulations. Well, he said, if I'm being honest I am already wondering how I'm going to get on with my life after I leave you.

She took the few steps toward him, she uphill and almost his own height on the trail, and she put her arms around his neck and looked at him. He returned her look steadily. He did not feel as panicked saying this as he had expected. He actually hadn't expected to say it at all, but having said it he was aware of anticipating either some evasive response, or her discomfort, or something else unknown but truly unfavorable. I know what you mean, she said.

You don't seem bothered by it at all.

She smiled very sweetly at him. Well, I'm just trying to enjoy the time we have together.

He nodded.

Come, she said. We're almost there. We can talk more at the beach, or better yet, in the water. I'm roasting. The ocean will fix everything.

She kissed him and then resumed her place before him and he found himself wretchedly torn between hope and despair and surrender.

On the beach, the same beach, just over twenty-four hours since she had come to sit beside him, the two of them in the same spot. Our spot, she had said. How cruel to assume possession of something on their collective behalf when the truth of the matter was actually that this was her beach and he was only visiting, and when he left, he would go back home as a different man entirely and that his heart would never really leave her, and that probably she would go on with her life like nothing had happened. He half-smiled and set down the bag he had carried. He pulled off his shirt and said he wanted to swim.

Well obviously, she said, smiling. That is why we've come, after all. As she said this she was shimmying down her shorts and peeling off her cover-up and something in the lithe movements of her tanned body softened him. When she was ready he watched her read the expression on his face. She stepped toward him and took his face in her hands. Hey, she said. The water will help.

How could it, he thought. How could it. It couldn't of course. Because water can't cancel flights, except for maybe weather if you counted that, or tsunamis, or floods, or oh what the hell. You're ruining this for both of you, he thought. Stop it. He closed his eyes, and drew a breath, and he could feel the salt in his nose and for the first time, somehow, since they had arrived at the beach, he heard the waves. He smiled involuntarily. He opened his eyes, and then he broke away from her and ran as fast as he could toward the surf, and he could hear her laughing joyfully behind him and then he felt the water envelop his feet and then his legs and the waves breaking against his knees and the perfect temperature of the water and the sand becoming gravel briefly beneath his feet as he ran and then the sand returning, irregular and topographic from the currents and then he stepped in a hole and fell forward into the water as a wave rose and salt water filled his nose and he clenched his eyes shut and when he came up the day was bright and perfect, and she was there beside laughing and pressing her hair back.

You are a wild man, she said, still laughing.

He looked at her, and looked around. At the water stretching to the horizon, at the hills descending down into the ocean, tree-covered and green against the cloudless sky. He saw, back on the shore, two children playing in the sand, burying one another and giggling. You were right, he said.

Oh? she asked.

The ocean does make everything better.

See? she said, grinning broadly. I told you. She splashed him and he dove toward her, his arms catching her waist and the two of them tumbling into the waves.

They swam as they had the day before, some spontaneous dance of contact and separation, of individuality and togetherness. The ocean some medium between them, some perfect equalizer, some mystic force of nature, of love, of being. In it they were perfect, and the feeling stayed with them as long as the last drops of that water remained on their skin.

On the beach they fell asleep and awoke to someone asking if they would donate to an organization that operated orphanages.

He was a very old man, dressed in a white button-down shirt and vaqueros, or jeans, and a white, western-style cowboy hat. He was clean-shaven and wore boots, and he had a rodeo belt buckle on.

He told them the story of a girl who had been staying with her grandmother while her parents emigrated to the United States to find work. They had been detained by immigration authorities several weeks in and were being held. And then her grandmother had become sick, and had died, and she had walked sixty kilometers to the nearest bus station and asked someone there for help and the orphanage had been contacted and she was there, awaiting the release of her parents should that ever come to pass, but otherwise alone. Damian listened to the story attentively and when it had finished he gave the man all the pesos he had in his wallet and asked for a website or address where he could give more than what he had on him at the time. The man shook his hand emphatically and called him a buen hombre and shook his hand again and told him, in English, that God would be with him. Then he went down the beach.

He sat a while after the man left and looked out at the sea. When Emilia sat up and ran her hand over his back and asked if he was alright he nodded. I think that story really affected me, he said.

She was silent but continued touching him. Then she said, I don't know if that story was true. But there are a lot of true stories like that.

He nodded, saying nothing.

It really puts our problems into perspective, doesn't it, he said after a while.

Yes. Do you still have both your parents?

He nodded. Y tú? he asked.

Ahh, very good! she praised. Then her face shifted, and she said that she had lost her mom when she was a teenager. Her eyes held the learned resignation and surrender of someone who has worked hard to overcome something very tragic. He had seen that look before. Not from her, but from other people. A sort of sad sincerity unknown except to those who had known it.

I'm sorry, he said. How old were you?

Sixteen, she said, smiling now. She was an amazing woman. My hero. And now, my martyr.

Your martyr? He wondered if this was one word she did not

really understand in English.

A gull landed on the beach before them and they both looked briefly at it. The wind blew stronger and the gull alighted and was gone.

Yes, of course, she said, smiling again. When she died I discovered in me this new freedom to become whatever I wanted to become. She died for my cause, I think. Not like I am responsible for her death or anything, or that she had to die to liberate me. That all sounds very dramatic when I explain it that way. No, more like because she lived so short a time, I feel like it is my responsibility as a daughter to live for her. To live what she was not able to live.

As he listened he recalled what she had said about moving around, living in different countries. He thought of all she had told him about her views on commitment and love and honesty and giving words to whatever arose in your heart and then he understood.

I think that's a very beautiful way of looking at it, he said, shifting his gaze from the sea to her.

She smiled sweetly. Thank you, she said. Kiss me.

And he did, and they reclined once again on the towel and did not sleep but laid each of them with their eyes closed and listened to the sounds of the beach. The vendedores left them alone and the breeze blew pleasantly and he felt the sun on his skin and the sand where it had dried on him and he felt her skin, too, and the rise and fall of her breath. He wondered if she would move to Idaho. Who was he to decide her next chapter. It seemed even she was not fully possessed of that ability. Then he sat up and said, I think I'm going to stay a little longer.

She was lying on her stomach now, her head turned toward him, and she opened her eyes. On the beach? she asked.

No, he said, rolling on his side to face her. Here. In Sayulita.

She closed her eyes again, still smiling. I think you've been drinking ocean water again.

Something in his chest clenched. No, he said. I mean it. I am so happy here. And you're right, life is so short. I can't imagine leaving this place when I feel so good here. Not yet anyway. And you, he thought. I can't bring myself to leave you. But he did not say it.

She rolled over and sat up and ran her fingers through her hair. Damian, she said. I know how you feel.

But what, he asked.

She sighed. I see what's happening.

What do you mean?

She paused, or hesitated, or put her thoughts together. He wasn't sure exactly what was going on in her mind, except that he felt as though she was formulating an escape plan and the clench in his chest tightened. This was how it was always going to go, he thought.

It's not about you, he said before she could speak. I mean I'm glad to have met you, obviously, but I really do feel like this is a place I would like to spend more time.

She laughed. Of course it's about me, she said. Inside her there had arisen such a strong feeling of entrapment that she could not explain. Had she not herself thought of his hand with a wedding ring just the night before? Had she not felt more safe with him than any other time in her life, especially than with any other man? I don't know, Damian. I just – you have a whole life in Idaho and I want you to stay here, but you can't stay here forever. You know that, and I know that.

So what, you feel like because it can't be forever it's not worth a few more days?

No, it's not that. I mean, yes, maybe it is.

He sat up and leaned forward on his knees. She rose slightly and propped herself up on her elbows.

He was brushing the sand from his ankles. You said yesterday that I should move here and then I could see you whenever I wanted.

Yes, she said, touching his hand, stilling his rapid movements, maybe. And I meant it then. I still mean it. It was a dream – a fantasy – it would be a beautiful thing.

Then why are you saying I shouldn't stay? He pulled his hand away from her and pulled his knees closer to his chest with his arms.

Because, it isn't supposed to be that way, she said after a moment, quietly.

He waited for her to go on but she did not. What do you mean Emilia? It isn't supposed to be this way.

I mean, I can't say it any other way. It's just what it is. You are not meant to stay here and I am not meant to move to America (how had she known he was thinking this at all, he wondered) and we are just a star in the sky – a bright point of light, and then we burn out. And it's okay, because it is beautiful while it lasts.

He rubbed his forehead with both hands as though in exasperation. Then he looked out at the bright clear skyline.

But I want it to last longer.

It struck him as he said this that it might have been the most honest and vulnerable words he had ever spoken.

She scooted closer to him on the blanket and kissed his shoulder. I do too, she said.

Then what are we doing, he asked.

We are having an argument when we only have a little bit more time together, she said into his skin. That was how it felt. As if she was speaking into his skin, into his body, into the parts of him that knew without knowing. The animal. The little boy who ran into the ocean freely, wildly. The man who had yet to emerge but was inside somewhere waiting to be fully awakened.

The statement stopped his thoughts. He was paused, cognitively paralyzed, and somehow the clench that had been in his chest, already loosened by her body beside his so close now, released the rest of the way with her words.

He nodded. I'm sorry, he said.

I am too.

He turned his head toward her and she kissed him and then she asked if he would like to swim once more before they walked home. He wanted to ask if he could stay with her that night but he did not ask. And she felt the question on the tip of his tongue as she stood and brushed the sand off her legs, and she smiled at him for not asking. But if he had asked, she thought, she would've said yes, even though she felt like saying that it would probably be better if they didn't. And in not asking, he had alchemized somehow her sense of entrapment and obligation and guilt, and had opened the door to her to choose instead for herself what she wanted, and in that space she realized that in fact she hoped for him to sleep beside her for one more night.

If he could stay this man. The confident, self-assured man. The man who loved her without needing to hold her too tightly. The man who trusted her. That was what it was, really. Trust. She needed him to trust her and to let her go, and to know that like a bird she would always come back. I am like a bird, she thought. How easily my bones are crushed.

They swam together again but this time for the most part they did not touch, and he did not reach for her, or follow her, or seem to need her near him at all, and at the same time he did not seem to be doing it out of spite. It was more like he was in his own world, thoughtful, reflective, present. With himself, and the moment. She liked that. She watched him secretively. Like she had the day before, before she had gone to talk to him. She sank beneath the water as a wave came and stayed beneath as long as her lungs would allow, listening to the wave breaking overhead, to the currents beneath and the way the water tousled the sand on the ocean floor, feeling the light in refracting brilliance beneath the surface of the water. She felt the stillness brought by the absence of breath, wondered if in the moment before death, after the heart has stopped, if there could be found a similar stillness. It was almost a pleasure to cease to be alive. The incredible peace. Una paz inexplicable, she thought. When she broke the surface he was floating on his back and she swam to him and she ran her fingers through his hair beneath the water and pulled his head to her chest and leaned forward and kissed his forehead. He smiled without opening his eyes.

Are you ready, she asked as he dropped to standing and wiped the water from his face. He opened his eyes and saw her there in the water, shining, golden in the sun, light off the water dancing across her face. He kissed her once on the mouth, and then parted with her and said, Yes.

They walked from the beach in near silence. At one point she said, Thank you. He asked for what, and she told him: For sharing your feelings with me. He almost said: I'm sorry I got emotional. He almost said: I'm sorry I ruined our afternoon. He almost said: Thank you. Finally, he said nothing, and they continued to walk.

When they reached his habitación he said he was going to shower and read for a bit and would she like to get dinner or a drink with him in a few hours. She almost invited him to come do those things at her house, felt some instantaneous but short-lived panic at the thought of parting with him, but did not ask him. She told him to come and get her when he was ready. He nodded, and kissed her, and stepped inside and shut the door.

As she walked away, she missed him. Savored, actually, the feeling of missing him. What a gift he had given her. To miss him. It burned like an ache in her chest and she savored it. To miss someone is to know that you love them. It was what her first boyfriend had said when he let her go. She didn't understand then – knew only that she had to go and felt certain as she left that she was ruining everything at the expense of her own convictions to live the life she was meant to live – but he had said that and she had known that he was right and she had loved him so much for it, because he had given her in that simple statement the peace that would get her through the following very hard months. How much he had taught her, really, about life and love. How good a man he had been. I have known so many good men, she thought.

After closing the door, he shed his shorts and walked immediately to the shower. And there he stood until the water ran cold, and then he remained there until something inside him decided it was time to get out. Who could say how long he had been under the water. It was selfish, he knew. In this place where water was so scarce, and expensive. But he needed it. He thought of the orphanage. Need – how varied the meanings for that word. He didn't need to stand in the shower. A child needed their parents. And he had gotten his, and those children probably never would. God, this world, he thought.

Once he had dried off he looked up the name of the orphanage the man on the beach had given. He could not remember the name exactly, but looked up regional organizations and found one that seemed to ring a bell. They were located to the south, almost in Puerto Vallarta, and he spent some time learning what he could from the internet, though he could not locate a website. For a moment during this time he had considered the relative anonymity of the developing world, especially compared to America. How in his circles it would be unthinkable for a reputable organization to not have a website. But how society continued to function here in the absence of so many allegedly necessary infrastructures, much as it had before the advent of the internet. People carried messages with them, histories were preserved in the stories told around the dinner table, phones used more for immediate and tactical communication than anything. Of course they still had social media here. He had seen children watching video shorts on a phone outside of a few of the tiendas and he had wondered what sorts of things the Spanish side of the internet held, compared to the English side. In this moment it struck him how large the world really was and how very little of it he actually knew.

As she had walked by one of the bars someone she knew had called to her and she had stopped in to say hello, had ended up sitting, and was currently drinking a beer.

El chisme es que tienes un novio, Yusuf said. He was an old friend of hers who had moved to Sayulita around the same time as her, he also speaking many languages, having moved first from a town outside Mumbai, and then lived in the Czech Republic, then Madrid, and now having moved to Mexico. He had always worked in tourism but said he preferred to work in bars because you learned more about the world that way. I learned that in Prague, he said.

You and your chisme, she said. They often spoke in English so he could practice, and because he said it made the American tourists more inclined to come in if the chatter was in a language they understood.

Well, is it true? he asked.

Why are you so interested, she asked. Do you have a crush on me or something.

A crush? he asked. I don't know this word. Crush.

It means do you feel el amor for me, she said smiling and taking a drink of her beer.

Por supuesto que sí, but that is not what is important here.

And that would be? she asked.

Well, is it true that you have a new boyfriend? he asked again. Here, take some tequila it will make you talk with me.

They say have some tequila, en ingles.

Fine, have some tequila, he said, pouring two shots.

I don't know, she said. I think I am going to see him tonight and I don't know if I feel like drinking yet.

Ah, you want to be fully present for tu amor. He rolled his r's emphatically.

Shhh, she said, and took the shot. Yes, if you must know, I met a man yesterday and I was out with him last night.

Ah! he exclaimed, slapping the bar top. Lo sabía!

Cállate la boca, she said, though she smiled as she said it and looked out at the street. It was cool in the bar with the fans on even though it was still a very hot day.

Pues, what is the name of this man?

His name is Damian. But I think it is hard for him to meet someone on vacation.

What do you mean, Yusuf asked. He does not like to give himself or?

Ha, she laughed. No, the opposite. He wants to stay, and love me forever.

Ah, well, you cannot blame him, he replied. What's not to love.

Mi amor, she said, affectionately. You do have a crush on me.

Yes, of course. Do you like him this same amount? Or maybe not?

I do like him, she said, sliding her fingers down the condensation on her beer bottle. I like him a lot.

Well, maybe it is those scarries coming back to get you.

What scarries, she asked, smiling again.

Oh you know, didn't this happen with that man in Indonesia? Who you said you were so in love with? And you just had to leave as you say?

Shhh you, she said. Then she paused. Yes, maybe it was something like that.

See, I think that maybe it is that you are a little bit afraid of the commitment. Is that the word? Commitment? She nodded. Yes, that maybe you are not so sure of yourself or you think it will hold you back in some way.

I am not afraid of commitment.

Well, then you are very committed to your freedom. Which is not so bad, except that eventually maybe you will get lonely?

This is true, she said. Can I have another beer?

Por supuesto, he said, fishing one out of the cooler and opening it for her. Dame la botella.

She exchanged bottles with him and released an aggravated sigh. Of course I'm afraid of commitment, she said. I know this. I don't know why I deny it. If you could hear my inner dialog, you would see. Is it better or worse to know everything happening inside of you?

Yusuf laughed genuinely. Yes, better of course, he said. Can you imagine not knowing. It would be like flying a plane without seeing.

Flying blind, she said, is the saying.

Yes, well, either way, he said. At least you can see it.

But it still controls what I do. Like I can see the feeling coming but I can't do anything to stop it.

That is very natural, I think.

He said today that he wants to stay longer and I told him all sorts of reasons he couldn't, but really I think that I just kind of panicked and thought what if he stays and we have a very happy life together but he hates himself – and hates me – in five years because we break up because sometimes people do, and then it is all my fault for ruining his perfectly happy life.

Yusuf thought for a moment, nodding, drinking a beer. Do you think he has a very happy life?

I don't know – he seems kind of uptight, really.

I don't know this word. Uptight.

Like, estresado, she said.

Ah, bueno. Well, and you said he is a man, yes?

As in, not a woman?

No, he replied laughing. As in not a boy. My point is he is old enough to make his own decisions.

She looked at him for a long moment. I guess so.

I think you care a lot for other people, and want everyone to be happy. I think you are afraid of doing the wrong thing, and hurting people. But I think sometimes you hurt people more because you act out of fear.

She looked at him for a long time. A water truck rumbled by on the street outside so loudly that it would've been impossible to hear her response anyway. She waited. It passed. So what do you think I should do? she asked.

I am glad you have asked, he said. I don't know.

A lot of good you are.

Well, I never claimed to be able to fix your problems, Chica, I only ask you what they are.

Qué útil, she said, rolling her eyes.

Hey, he said. Es mi chisme.

I should go, she said. I need to shower and I think he will probably come to my house before long to get me for dinner.

Of course. What are you going to tell him?

She pushed a breath through her lips. No sé. I guess I'm just going to feel it and see what he says.

Okay, you go do your feeling. Feel this man you love so much. Give him many besos y tell him you love for him to be happy.

Ay cabrón!

You came in here on your own, you remember.

And I wonder why I do it every time.

Buena suerte Chica, he called after her as she left.

He closed his computer and saw that the light was quickly fading outside. The sun had shifted into evening, though it had not yet set. He looked at the time on his phone. 6:30 pm. He slid his finger across the screen and tapped a few icons and it began ringing.

Hey bud, said a voice on the other end.

Hey, am I bothering you?

Never. Just cooking some dinner for the kids. What's up? How's your tropical vacation?

It's good. I love it here.

Wow, you love it there? I actually didn't think you would ever say that.

Why not?

Because it's a developing country and you like systems that work.

Systems do work here. They're just... different systems.

I guess.

Have you ever been to Mexico?

No, except when we were kids and we used to visit Juarez with the family.

You should come sometime. Bring the kids. The beaches here are amazing.

You're north of Puerto Vallarta, right?

Yes.

Maybe someday. They're too little right now to enjoy it though.

That's fair. How are they, by the way?

Oh, wily as ever. Everett shit his pants and then pulled the curtains down on himself.

Ah, hiding behind them again I assume?

Yeah, I don't know why he does that.

It won't last.

I hope you're right.

I'm always right.

So have you met any chicas, or have you just been staying in your room?

I can tell you think so highly of my social skills.

That's not an answer.

Actually I did meet someone.

There's a silence on the line. The sounds of water running in the background. A kid crying. Then the voice says: Hang on one second.

Damian can hear his brother calling for his wife to help the crying child. Is that Esther?

Yeah, how'd you know?

She does that shriek thing when she cries. I don't think I've heard Everett do that.

He'll learn. Give him time. Okay, so wait what? You actually met someone?

Yeah, is that so hard to believe?

No, of course not. I'm just giving you a hard time. Who is she?

Her name is Emilia. She lives here.

Ahh, a local!

She's not from here originally. She's lived a bunch of places. I don't actually know where she's from originally. Maybe France or something.

And she speaks English?

Very well, actually. And Spanish. She seems to know everyone in this town.

She sounds like the opposite of you.

You have no idea.

What?

She's just a very free spirit.

Look at you branching out.

Well. The problem is I think I'm in love with her.

That's just vacation brain. You're not in love with her, you're just in love with the feeling you have right now and you don't want to come back to reality.

But how do you know this isn't reality? I'm living it, after all. How could it not be reality.

Well, but you can't live on the beach forever. You've got a job here that you can't do there. And you don't speak the language. And it's a foreign country. How would you even move there?

I could, probably. Do my job remotely to some degree. I wouldn't have to work as much since it's so much cheaper here. And I could learn the language.

You're actually thinking about it.
Yeah, I guess I am. I hadn't really realized I'd thought about it.
A pause.
Well, you sound happy. Relaxed.
I am, man. I feel really good here. I don't know if I said that before.
You did. Or I felt it, I don't know.
A pause.
Well your flight leaves tomorrow night, doesn't it? What are you going to do.
I have no idea. The thing is I brought up the idea of staying a few extra days and she kind of freaked out.
Like what do you mean?
I mean she said I shouldn't, and it wouldn't work, and neither of us is going to move and so why make it harder to say goodbye, or something like that. I think she's kind of avoidant.
Or you just completely misread the situation.
Or that. I've wondered that. I don't know though – there's something in the way she looks at me. She said yesterday, playfully, that she was trying to convince me to move here so I could see her whenever I wanted.
She sounds a little bit crazy.
I think she is and I think I like it. Like, people here love her, so she can't be that crazy, right? Truly crazy people have a hard time maintaining solid friendships.
You have a hard time maintaining solid friendships.
You're a pain in the ass.
There's that elegant charm again.
I mean it, though. I don't think she's really crazy. Just like, very carefree, you know? Anyway, she also said my hand would look good in a wedding ring.
Jesus Christ.
I know.
And you feel the same way about her.
I really like her. I think I love her.
You haven't... told her that, have you?
A pause.
Damian, you haven't told her you love her.
I did. It slipped out while we were having sex.

Oh fuck, you're a goner.

Shut up! She wasn't bothered. She said she thinks people should speak what's alive in their hearts, or something like that.

She is crazy. You know what, you two sound perfect for each other. She's crazy, you're usually very level-headed. But she's now making you crazy, too, which sounds to me like the hallmark of a great relationship.

You're so helpful.

As always.

So what do I do?

You're asking me for advice?

Unfortunately for me, yes.

Well, I think you should come home tomorrow and get your head on straight. You can always go back. If it's real, what you feel between the two of you, then it will be something you can pick up again, or keep alive by phone or whatever. Then if you still feel the same way about each other after a few weeks or months or however long, you can go back to visit. You have time, you know, to figure it out.

That's actually really good advice.

And you doubted me.

Never. Well, yes.

A pause.

Damian.

Yeah.

I'm happy for you man. It does sound a little crazy, but life is crazy sometimes.

Thanks.

Yeah. Hey, I better go. Dinner is about done and the kids are about to eat each other if I don't feed them.

Can't have that. Little cannibals.

Thanks for calling. Good to talk to you.

Thanks for talking. It helped.

Good.

Love you bud.

You too, see you later.

He tapped the red button and ended the call, then put his phone face-down on the table. It was just past seven.

El Desenlace

She was painting her toenails when she heard a knock on the door. She called for him to come in and said she was in her room. She heard the door open and he called out into the space, saying: Hello, am I interrupting?

No, of course not, she said. I'm just in here and can't get up.

He wondered what on earth she could mean, and when he turned the corner of the room he saw her sitting on the end of the bed interminably focused on her task, her tongue sticking out the side of her mouth in concentration. When his shape came into her view she looked up and smiled brightly at him. Hello, you, she said.

Hello, he said.

Kiss me.

He did. That's a beautiful color, he said, admiring her toes from where he stood beside the bed. They match this.

He produced a yellow trompeta flower that he had picked on his way over. For me? she asked, looking up at him through her eyelashes. He nodded. She sniffed it and closed her eyes for a moment, and then asked if he would put it behind her ear. He did this, and she leaned toward him again for a kiss.

I want to talk to you about what we were talking about earlier, she said.

It's okay, he replied. I've cleared my head. I'm sorry I was getting caught up.

Oh, I was going to say I was sorry I reacted so poorly to what was actually a very normal idea. Not normal in the way that most people would think of it, but I think given the circumstances I could ha—

He kissed her again, and she smiled against his lips. It's okay, he said. It's really okay. Let's just focus on tonight.

When he pulled back he found her gazing at him with something that to him looked like admiration. He took this image in his mind and hoped to God he could remember it just like it happened. Just like this, he thought. Okay, she said.

And we are going to pretend that I am staying forever. But it's just pretend. He looked directly into her eyes. Just pretend, he said again. So don't worry, okay?

She continued looking up at him, half the toes on her right foot painted, the other half not, and she nodded very solemnly without breaking his eye contact. Okay, she said.

He reached in his pocket and produced a cheap golden ring from one of the vendor stands on the plaza and told her she could put it on him if she wanted.

Are you asking me to pretend marry you? she asked.

I am. Will you?

I will, she said, and she took the ring and placed it on his left ring finger. What will I wear? she asked.

He produced a comically large ring with a plastic gemstone, and handed it to her. She laughed out loud.

It's perfect. I've always wanted a huge ring that told everyone exactly how much money I have.

This is perfect then, because if we really were getting married we would probably end up being very poor with the way you would ruin our finances.

I would not! she decried.

You're always doing this, he said, insinuating an almost believable irritation.

I've always loved our lovers' quarrels, she said then laying her head on his forearm.

Mi amor, he said. She smiled.

How much longer do you need to be ready? he asked.

Not long. Just these few toes and then I will put on some respectable clothes and we can go. Where are we going, by the way?

Do you like Mediterranean food?

I do!
Good, because we have a reservation there in fifteen minutes.
Where?
The tall place, I forget what it was called.
She giggled. Alto Alto, sí?
Yes, that's the one.
Well what would you have done if I wasn't ready to go?
I told them on the phone that we might be late because my girl-friend takes forever to get ready. So they gave me three reservations for every fifteen minutes beginning with this first one, in fifteen minutes.
She was grinning uncontrollably at him now.
And if I didn't like Mediterranean food?
I would have taken you to the Italian place where I also have a reservation.
Just one?
Yes, just one there, in thirty minutes.
Oh, and if I didn't like Italian?
Then I would have eaten Mediterranean food by myself and let you enjoy your narrow tastes in peace, but alone.
She threw her head back in a laugh. You are very good to me, my husband.
Anything for my beautiful esposa.
Ahh you learned a new word!
He kissed her on the head and told her he would wait out front.
You don't want to watch me get dressed?
No, he said as he walked from the room. We have dinner plans and we cannot afford to be delayed.
But we can, she said after him. Because you said you made three reservations.
It's not polite, he said through the wall. Vamos.

He ordered for them both this time, and she wore her gaudy ring all night, and over dinner they talked about the orphanage he had looked up and what he had learned, and they talked about global poverty and how the richest nations seemed to handle it with incredible incompetence, at least from a government standpoint, except for the Scandinavian countries, she commenting that they seemed to do everything very well and the two of them wondering what it was about those countries that seemed to thrive amongst the same challenges of human greed that apparently caused the rest of the world to flounder.

He said the word flounder, and she did not know it, and so he explained what it meant and she called him very intelligent.

I'm not really, he said finishing the last of his drink.

You are, though. Did you know that last night when you were talking about water rights and things like that—

I didn't even think you were listening to me, he interjected.

I was. I mean I was distracted, but it was because I was thinking to myself how intelligent and conscientious you are.

Well, you did marry me for a reason, he replied, touching her thigh through her linen pants.

I did, she said, smiling. I can't believe how quickly the time has gone. It feels as though we just met yesterday.

I know, how time flies when you're in love.

You do love me, then? she asked, looking up into his face. You haven't changed your mind with all my outbursts?

And he looked at her and he smiled and said of course he hadn't changed his mind. I have never met anyone like you.

Nor have I, she said.

He did not say he was going to miss her. He did not say that he would never forget her. Tonight was, he had decided, outside of time and space. He would not miss her, because in the container of tonight, he would have her forever.

In his eyes she read the pain he felt from loving her. She felt the way it moved him. And she admired his strength in constructing this night for the two of them in spite of the way it must have hurt him.

Can we go home? she asked then.

He smiled, kindly, genuinely, happily, she thought, and nodded. Then he called for the bill.

In the morning they woke without an alarm after 8:00am and it had rained in the night and they could smell it on the air. She did not go to yoga, and he did not get up to leave, and they stayed in bed together all through the morning. After they had made love, sweetly, softly, quietly, whispering almost to each other with their bodies alone, their skin like secrets each kept for the other, she said from her place resting on his chest, that if he stayed, she would be happy.

He felt himself smiling almost overflowing with emotion. You just want me for the sex, he said.

Mhmm, she replied. It's very good.

But that's not all, she added after a moment.

Even as he smiled, there arose a conflict of feeling within him. It might have been that he found it hard to trust her whims, since they seemed always to be changing. It might have been the uneasy feeling that comes when someone is very close to getting something they want very deeply, like a preemptory sort of pain from having and losing. Or it might've been simply the conflict between love and responsibility, knowing that even if he wanted to stay, realistically he couldn't.

I do want to stay, he said.

Then stay. You can stay with me.

He felt these words deep in his stomach.

I can't he replied.

I know, she said then.

But I can come back soon.

He felt her smile against his chest.

How soon?

I don't know. Maybe in a month. Maybe sooner. There are direct flights. I may not be able to come for a week or anything, but I could come for a long weekend. I can actually do some of my work here.

We don't have to figure it all out now, she said quietly. You will come back, and I will be here. And then we can be married again. You will be my American husband.

Stay here, she instructed, rising from the bed.

She stepped lightly over the piles of clothes on the floor to the bookshelf and pulled down an old polaroid camera. Then she sat again beside him on the bed. Look like you love me, she said, and snapped a picture before he could respond.

He had been looking at her, and she at the camera, she smiling and he gazing at her like she was the best thing in the world to happen to him.

Then she kissed him and took another.

She handed him the camera and told him to take one of her without clothes on. He did this, and she refused to look at it, but he thought it was the most beautiful picture of any person he'd ever seen. He glanced at the clock on the stove.

I'd better be going, he said. My car is going to be here in an hour and I have to pack.

What if I could take you, she asked.

What, on the motorbike? he chuckled.

No, por supuesto que no. My friend Aditi has a truck and she could drive the two of us to the airport and I could ride back with her.

He considered this for a minute. I can pay her for gas and her time, he offered.

She would gladly accept gas money, but she won't accept money for her time.

He smiled. And you want to do this? And she won't mind?

She owes me a favor or two anyway, Emilia said, grinning. I set her up with her husband.

Ah, and now it is her turn, eh?

Something like that, she said, kissing him on the mouth and rising from the bed. Though it's not the same since we're already married.

You wait a few minutes and I'll put on clothes and we can both go to your place to pack. I can help you.

Oh no, he said. You're not helping me pack. I've seen your closet. You are a tornado. How do you say storm in Spanish?

She squinted at him, wrinkling her nose. Tormenta, she said. La tormenta.

La Nota

He didn't find the note in his suitcase until he had arrived home and was loading his clothes into the laundry. It was a piece of paper ripped from her journal, dated on one side from the day before, with the words la tarde written beside the date. It was written in Spanish. On the other side was a note in English.

Paperclipped to the note was the polaroid he had taken of her, and the one of the two of them kissing. He looked at the photos for a long minute, feeling the most intensely opposed emotions all at once – pain and joy, sorrow and elation, gratitude and resentment, fear and hope – and then he read the note:

Keep these so you don't forget how beautiful I am. I wrote this journal entry about you, but you're going to have to work on your Spanish to read it. No cheating! Call me when you make it home. I will see you soon.

Below she had written her phone number.

So you don't forget how beautiful I am. What a menace. As if he would ever forget. It would be impossible. Impossible. What are you doing, he thought to himself, smiling irrepressibly. Jesus Christ. Jesus Christ.

Tormenta

Español

La Playa

Él abrió el libro y lo primero que vio fue el trozo de papel de recibo en la vigésima página, de la última vez que había empezado a leerlo. ¿Hacía cuántos años fue eso? Probablemente la última vez que tomó unas vacaciones. Eso tenía sentido. ¿Dos años ya? ¿Cinco? Una nube se movió en el cielo y la página se oscureció y él oyó el sonido de las olas rompiendo y se dio cuenta de que no podía ver la página con sus gafas de sol puestas ahora que el cielo había cambiado. Se las quitó y las posicionó en la parte superior de su cabeza. Saco el marcapáginas de su lugar y lo puso más atrás, con la intención de leer más allá de la página 20 esta vez. La gente lee libros durante las vacaciones, ¿cierto? Él era una de esas personas, había decidido. Hacía mucho tiempo. Siempre había sido una de esas personas. Algunas personas leen todo el tiempo. ¿Quién tiene tiempo para eso? Sin embargo durante las vacaciones - por placer. Leer sería un placer.

Se enfocó de nuevo y leyó la primera página. Era un estrecho libro de tapa blanda, que había encontrado en una de esas bibliotecas callejeras cerca de la playa. En sus últimas vacaciones, recuerda. Hemingway - El viejo y el mar. Se doblaba y retorcía con la suave brisa, las páginas revoloteando bajo su pulgar. El leve sonido del papel crujiendo. Qué agradable. Él podía oler el océano - el océano de verdad más allá de la playa. La arena bajo él era cálida en los dedos de sus pies, donde colgaban más allá de la toalla. Podía oler el mar, y le gustaba. La sal, y el ligero olor oceánico. ¿Qué era eso? ¿Qué lo hacía oler de ese modo? Más leve aquí que en otros lugares. Seattle, por ejemplo – había estado allí, y el océano olía antiguo y profundo, y de algún modo más penetrante que este mar. Y él estaba más cerca aquí. Tal vez no era tanto el océano en sí mismo en Seattle sino el puerto. La ciudad. Probablemente era eso. Inhaló profundamente y volvió a la página.

Las nubes se movieron de nuevo y la página brilló como retroiluminada por la luz radiante y limpia, y la miró entrecerrando los ojos por un momento intentando seguir leyendo, decidido a evitar las distracciones. Maldición, qué brillante, pensó. Se puso sus gafas de sol de nuevo. Había una mancha en la esquina. La ignoró por un momento y luego colocó el libro sobre su muslo y encontró su camisa entre sus cosas a su lado y se quitó las gafas y las limpió a su satisfacción y luego se las puso de nuevo y retomó el libro. Por eso nunca leo, pensó. Jesucristo.

Una ola rompió y algunos niños jugando en el océano chillaron. Se gritaron los unos a los otros en español. No podía entenderles. No realmente. Reconocía una frase aquí y allá. Inflexión infantil sobre palabras sencillas. Algo sobre su entusiasmo captó su atención, le hizo sonreír, mirando suavemente en su dirección sin verlos de verdad. Ese sonido era algo – el sonido de las olas. El océano vivo, casi. La creciente estática de la ola y luego la cresta y el rompiente como una gran liberación, y sus voces — las voces de los niños — ganando mientras él imaginaba la gran campana azul verdosa de la ola elevándose desde la superficie y doblándose sobre sí misma y luego la imaginó rompiendo sobre sus cabezas mientras ellos reían abrumados de alegría, el océano poderoso más allá de su comprensión, pero gentil con ellos. Amable, el océano. Y otras veces despiadado y horrible. Él volvió a su lectura.

Era un libro lento de empezar. No era gran cosa como libro, realmente, al menos en cuanto a su longitud — fue atrevido por parte de Hemingway, empezar un libro breve tan despacio. O quizá él no era un lector muy bueno. Había oído eso antes — que algunas personas simplemente no tienen la comprensión inmediata o la capacidad de concentración o la atención a los detalles para disfrutar de la lectura. Él estaba disfrutando del libro, ¿Qué significaba eso? Qué a menudo la gente escapa los confines de sus supuestas cajas. Él no estaba seguro de todas formas, honestamente, si estaba disfrutando del libro o solo disfrutando el acto de leer. De estar en la playa y leyendo. Las nubes se habían dispersado del todo ahora y el sol era brillante sobre su cabeza y él se había puesto cómodo en la toalla por fin y estaba cálido y el aire olía agradable y él podía entender cómo alguien - alguien que leyera mucho - podría disfrutar mucho de algo como esto. De esto exactamente, pensó él. Esto era. Esto era leer. Se percató de que había perdido su lugar en la página — había estado leyendo sin leer de verdad — y retrocedió y encontró dónde había perdido la concentración y retomó la lectura.

Un anciano y un niño hablando. El niño era muy amable y el anciano también. Ya no hay relaciones como esas, pensó. Tal vez no en los Estados Unidos. ¿Quizás en México? En Cuba donde el libro estaba ambientado. Se preguntó cuán similar era Cuba a México. Le gustaba México. Los niños aún estaban en las olas jugando y riendo. Se percató de la cabeza de una mujer en el agua, también, subiendo y bajando con las olas. Lejos de los niños - no con ellos, pensó para sí. No era su madre, probablemente. Ninguno de los niños la llamó.

Ella había estado flotando sobre su espalda, pero había salido a la superficie cuando él la había mirado por casualidad. Él pensó que quizá ella había mirado en su dirección, quizá había sostenido su mirada. Probablemente no - probablemente ella no le había visto de todos modos. Se imaginó que era muy hermosa — imaginándolo, porque ella estaba demasiado lejos como para que él pudiera verla de verdad. Pero se sentía como si ella fuera muy hermosa. Qué extraña proyección, pensó. Por supuesto que pensarías eso. Ella se giró, su cabello negro, brillando en el sol, y miró hacia el océano abierto. Su imagen estaba ligeramente oscurecida por las ondas de calor en la atmósfera. Por el reflejo del sol en la superficie del agua, como los flashes de las viejas películas de conciertos famosos, o como luciér-nagas. Él se dió cuenta de que estaba sonriendo, mirando la página sin ver. Miró el número de la página. Veintiséis - eso era mejor que la última vez. Un chico se acercó y le preguntó si quería comprar algunos camarones en una brocheta. Él determinó que eran shrimp y supuso que habían sido marinados y asados a la parrilla, y tenían un color naranja y un aspecto apetecible bajo el sol brillante. La playa dorada, el océano de un color turquesa intenso, el camarón naranja y el verde de la lima sobre el camarón en la brocheta. Más allá del chico vendiendo los camarones, en un suave foco, la cabeza de la mujer que él había visto, cabello negro y resplandeciente en el sol. El hombre preguntó si los camarones eran picantes, intentando recordar la palabra en español para eso. ¿Estas caliente? preguntó él. El chico se rió de buen humor. Spicy? Preguntó el chico. Él sintió que tal vez se había sonrojado, y asintió. No really, unless you want, el chico respondió en un inglés chapucero, sosteniendo una botella de salsa picante. Un poquito, dijo el hombre, haciendo un gesto de pellizco con los dedos. El chico asintió con gravedad, como si el tema del picante fuera muy serio. El hombre preguntó que cuánto era. Cuarenta, dijo el chico, o tres por cien pesos. Cuánto es eso, pensó para sí el hombre. Dos dólares. O tres por cinco. Asintió, rebuscó en su bolsillo, produjo unos cuantos billetes y se los entregó y el chico guardó el dinero en su bolsillo y salpicó algo de salsa picante en cada uno de los camarones en la brocheta, y luego se la entregó al hombre donde estaba sentado en la arena. El chico le agradeció al hombre y luego pasó a la siguiente persona en la playa, la misma interacción repetida de nuevo como si algún pliegue en el tiempo hubiera producido el mismo escenario pero con un actor diferente. El hombre olió el camarón ensartado en la brocheta y cerró los ojos, olía muy bien. Exprimió la lima sobre ellos, inclinando el brazo y la brocheta sobre la arena para no gotear sobre su toalla, y luego se los comió y encontró que estaban muy, muy buenos. Buscó al chico una vez se los hubo comido todos, pensando que quizá compraría dos más después de todo, pero el chico se había ido. Cuando sus ojos volvieron de recorrer la playa con la mirada, él la vio a ella saliendo del agua.

La mujer de antes. Ella estaba caminando, estaba saliendo del agua. Él se quedó inmóvil, observándola. Él había practicado no mirar fijamente a las mujeres, cada vez que había visto una muy hermosa había practicado intencionadamente el arte de no quedarse mirándola boquiabierto. Una mirada era perdonable, pero quedarse mirando – eso era comportarse como un puerco. Era grosero y objetivador. Él no era esa clase de persona. Tuvo amigos que eran de esa manera, y le disgustaban. Pero con ella no podía evitarlo. Y ella le devolvió la mirada. Saliendo del agua, sonriendo levemente; al principio, ella había tenido los ojos cerrados, sus manos quitando el agua de su cabello, gotas de lluvia formándose en su piel y corriendo en regueros por su cuerpo, y él se sintió tan celoso del agua durante ese breve instante y luego instantáneamente avergonzado por un pensamiento así de intrusivo - el pensamiento se sentía intrusivo en el espacio personal de ella, su propio cuerpo. Ella había quitado el agua de su cabello y él la había observado, y los ojos de ella estaban cerrados como si estuviera saboreando la forma en que el sol la envolvía, sol y agua compitiendo por ella. Para tocarla. Y los ojos de él, empujados de alguna manera a esta batalla. ¿Y dónde estaba ella? En el medio, y disfrutándolo. Sí, de algún modo él tuvo la impresión de que ella amaba ser el premio en algún sentido. O quizás era solo que ella amaba la armonía que sentía con todo a su alrededor. Dios, qué estaba pasando en su cabeza, él se preguntó. Y entonces ella estaba abriendo los ojos, despacio, deleitándose, sus caderas moviéndose mientras caminaba sin esfuerzo fuera del agua, su altura aumentando a medida que avanzaba por la playa. Sus ojos se estaban abriendo y entonces le vio mirándola y ella sonrió y no apartó la mirada por lo que realmente se sintió como una eternidad. Ella caminó, y caminó, y caminó hacia él, y él la observó, y la observó, y la observó, y ella le miró como si ya le amara y entonces ella pasó junto a él y él no movió la cabeza pero la siguió con la mirada. Él estaba tratando de decidir si darse la vuelta y ver a dónde había ido, pero aún no había podido atreverse a hacerlo cuando su voz, debía haber sido su voz, dijo casualmente: ¿Es ese El viejo y el mar?

Él miró el libro aún abierto en sus manos - ¿Qué habían estado haciendo sus manos todo este tiempo? Aparentemente nada — y asintió. Estaba casi a punto de hablar cuando ella apareció a su lado y comenzó a sentarse al lado de su toalla. Torpemente, de repente, como un súbdito que deja paso a una reina, él se apartó hacia un lado, como con diferencia, como por respeto a su aura, y logró ofrecerle un espacio en la toalla. Ella se rió de buen humor y se sentó en la arena. Él no podía evitar mirar la forma en la que la arena se aferraba a la piel desnuda en la parte trasera de sus muslos. La arena, ahora en la mezcla, también — arena, sol, agua, su mirada, qué elenco. Me encanta ese libro, dijo ella entonces, quitando el resto del agua de las puntas de su largo cabello negro. Él se percató entonces de lo largo que era su cabello. Le llegaba casi a la mitad de la espalda. No es que ella fuera alta. Pero tenía mucho cabello y era increíblemente bella. Sus ojos, también. Jesucristo, pensó él. No mires demasiado de cerca, nunca te recuperarás. Y aquí estaba ella sentada y hablándole a él.

No he avanzado mucho, dijo él entonces, mirando hacia abajo

como recordando por primera vez desde que ella había aparecido que tenía el libro. No es una lectura difícil ni nada parecido, yo solo...

Yo nunca puedo leer en la playa, dijo ella sin esperar a que él terminara. Ella tenía las rodillas levantadas y los codos, envueltos alrededor de ellas, inclinándose hacia delante de un modo relajado, como si estuviera a punto de comer una jugosa pieza de fruta y no quisiera que el jugo goteara en su regazo. Estaba mirando el océano, la arena aferrándose a la parte superior de sus muslos donde ella se había sentado al principio. No era una forma muy femenina de sentarse, pero había algo perfecto en ello. En ella. Te estás poniendo sentimental porque ella es una chica bonita dándote su atención, se dijo a sí mismo. No, pensó él entonces, ella era perfecta. ¿Por qué no lees en la playa? preguntó él.

Simplemente no puedo, dijo ella, quitando su mirada del horizonte para encontrarse con los ojos de él. Ella estaba sonriendo. Una sonrisa pícara y cómplice. Hay demasiado que ver, que sentir, supongo.

¿Demasiado que sentir?

Ella rió amablemente, suavemente. Sí, ¿No piensas lo mismo? Pasó los dedos por la arena y le contó que encontraba la playa muy sensual. Solamente, ella especificó, muy estimulante para los sentidos, ¿sabes? No sé si estoy usando las palabras correctas. No siempre conozco las palabras correctas en inglés, dijo ella. A él le pareció detectar cierta vergüenza en su voz cuando dijo eso.

Sé lo que quieres decir, dijo él. Para ser sincero creo que yo también he estado un poco distraído.

¿Oh? preguntó ella, alzando una ceja. ¿Algo en particular?

¿Está ligando conmigo? se preguntó él. Bueno, tú, por ejemplo, dijo él en voz alta y luego se preguntó por qué lo había dicho.

Hm, dijo ella sin dudar ni un solo segundo. ¿Soy una buena distracción, o una mala? Le estaba mirando directamente ahora. Cómo podía estar tan relajada, pensó él.

Él sentía calor por todo el cuerpo. Logró reírse ahogadamente. Supongo que tendremos que averiguarlo, dijo. ¿De dónde había salido eso? se preguntó. ¿Qué le estaba haciendo ella? Él nunca hablaba así.

Ella dejó escapar una risa gloriosa, sonora, fácil. Se rió mirando al cielo y el cielo le devolvió la risa. ¿Cómo hizo eso? Bueno, dijo ella entonces, ya lo veremos. ¿De dónde vienes?

Él dudó, sin saber por qué. Estados Unidos, dijo. Idaho.

Idaho, ella preguntó: Oh, allí hay patatas, ¿Cierto?

Hey, dijo él, más que patatas. Muchas montañas y bosques y lagos. Es muy hermoso. Pero no como esto.

No, dijo ella. Imagino que no. Esto es algo especial. Esta playa podría ser mi lugar favorito en el mundo. Es un gran riesgo para mí, sabes. Hablar contigo aquí. Justo aquí. ¿Y si me lo arruinas?

Jamás lo haría, dijo él.

No, dijo ella casi con nostalgia. No a propósito. Pero soy tu distracción, y tú eres mi riesgo, supongo. Qué emocionante. Ella puso una cara como si acabara de descubrir un secreto que la hacía feliz.

¿Cómo te llamas?

Emilia, contestó ella. ¿Y tú?

Damian, dijo él entonces. Mucho gusto, dijo ella extendiendo su mano, y él se incorporó ligeramente para estrechársela. Un placer conocerte, contestó él. ¿Y vives aquí?

Ella asintió. Desde hace unos años. No para siempre, probablemente. Pero por ahora, está bien.

¿Adónde más irías?

Hmm... Ella pasó los dedos por la arena a ambos lados de sí, trazando círculos en el arco que formaban sus brazos, como alas, o pétalos abriéndose hacia fuera desde donde estaba sentada. Bueno, antes estaba en Lisboa, en Portugal. He pasado algún tiempo en Malta. Y en Bali. No lo sé – ningún lugar en particular viene a mi mente ahora mismo. Pero seguro que habrá algún otro lugar. Quién sabe qué nos impulsa en nuestras vidas, ¿Sabes?

Él le dijo que a menudo se había sentido como si hubiera un montón de predeterminación en su vida, y le preguntó si ella no tenía algún tipo de plan para lo que ella quería.

¿Un plan? Preguntó ella, levantando las cejas. Lo dijo como si fuera una pregunta ridícula. Como si nadie en su sano juicio pusiera estructura alrededor de una vida. No, ningún plan. ¿Qué sentido tendría? ¿Acaso los planes salen bien? ¡Y la vida es tan corta!

A veces sí, dijo él. Los planes, quiero decir. Al menos para mí.

Bueno, me alegro por ti, respondió ella tras un momento. Dime pues, ¿Qué planes han funcionado para ti? Tengo mucha curiosidad.

Era el tipo de cosa que podría haber sonado acusatoria o despectiva o especulativa, pero no sonó de esa manera saliendo de sus labios. Ella estaba por completo, como dijo, intrigada.

Pues, fui a la escuela para estudiar negocios, que era lo que había planeado, y me las he arreglado para darme una buena vida a mí mismo con mi trabajo.

Ella lo observó, escuchando.

Soy un asesor empresarial, añadió él sin haber sido preguntado. Ayudo a empresas que no funcionan bien, y en cierto modo, las arreglo. Suena arrogante, pero no es mi intención. No es como si yo fuera un trabajador milagroso. En realidad, la mayoría de lo que hago es ayudar a la gente a hacer planes. Entonces él se rió entre dientes, por la coincidencia y el rumbo de la conversación. ¿A qué te dedicas tú?

Soy una artista. Hago tatuajes.

Él la miró fijamente por un momento. Como si esperara que continuase. Que dijera más. Que añadiera algo a eso. Pero se dió cuenta de que eso era todo lo que ella iba a decir al respecto.

¿Y ganas lo suficiente para vivir con eso?

Ella se río con esa risa brillante y fácil de nuevo. Sí, lo hago. Ella empujó el hombro de él juguetonamente, y cuando la mano de ella tocó su piel él sintió una oleada de euforia, como la primera calada a un cigarrillo.

Te hiciste tus propios tatuajes, él preguntó.

Algunos, dijo ella. Hice mis piernas. Algunos otros aquí y allá. Pero el resto han sido hechos por amigos, otros artistas. Es muy difícil tatuarse la propia espalda.

Él se sintió tonto por preguntar. Bueno, a mí me gustan todos, dijo él.

Gracias, dijo ella, colocándose un mechón de cabello tras su oreja.

¿Tienes algún tatuaje? ella preguntó.

No, dijo él. Siempre me ha preocupado que podrían no gustarme más tarde.

Ah, Damian, el planeador, dijo ella afectuosamente. Él se preguntó si ella era tan cercana con todas las personas que conocía. Tan amistosa. Deberías dejarme tatuarte, dijo ella.

Él pensó en ello, instantáneamente, como el destello de una idea, él tumbado allí sobre su espalda, o sobre su estómago, ella con sus herramientas produciendo su arte en el lienzo de su cuerpo. Él sonrió, pero no respondió. Se lo permitiría, si llegara a eso.

Cómo te hiciste tatuadora, preguntó.

Mi novio de hace muchos años era un tatuador. Hizo algunos de estos – aquí ella señaló sus brazos – bajo el codo, y mis manos. Hizo todos los tatuajes tradicionales. Esto era en Bali. Todos están hechos con una aguja de bambú y tinta natural, un pinchazo a la vez. Había todo un ritual alrededor de ello, es una práctica muy sagrada, ya sabes.

Mientras ella hablaba de esto, parecía ponerse sentimental. Hizo una pausa.

De todos modos, me fascinó, y como ya era una artista durante mucho tiempo, lo consideré simplemente como otro tipo de arte, pero en un lienzo vivo. Casi como hacer dibujos de arena. Pero más duraderos. Honestamente, estaba muy enamorada de él, y me interesaba todo lo que le interesaba, así que no es sorprendente que quisiera aprender. Afortunadamente él me enseñó muy bien, y yo era bastante buena en ello, y él me dió su bendición cuando me fui para continuar con la práctica por mi cuenta, aunque nos estábamos separando.

¿Por qué rompisteis?

Oh, no pienso en ello de ese modo. Solo estábamos juntos y luego tuvimos que separarnos. Era momento de seguir adelante para mí, podía sentirlo en mis huesos. Y él lo entendió – me dijo que debería irme, de hecho.

Aquí ella sonrió y echó su cabello hacia atrás por encima del hombro.

He sido muy afortunada de conocer a algunos hombres muy buenos.

Eso no es algo que se escuche todos los días.

¿No? preguntó ella, pareciendo genuinamente sorprendida.

Ja, de hecho no – siento que mucho de lo que escucho son historias de horror sobre los hombres siendo cerdos.

¿Crees que los hombres son cerdos? Tú no, obviamente.

No, no creo que los hombres sean cerdos. Algunos de nosotros, sí. Pero no todos.

¿Nadas? preguntó ella después de un breve lapso de silencio.

¿Quieres decir si sé nadar? preguntó él en respuesta.

Bueno, asumí que sabes nadar, ¿Aunque quizá no debería? Quería preguntarte si te gustaría venir a nadar conmigo. Me estoy sobrecalentando sentada aquí en la playa. Secándome como un lagarto.

Ella se levantó y se frotó la parte trasera de sus muslos, la arena cayendo como una suave lluvia, despacio y de alguna manera cinematográfica. Él observaba. Bueno, dijo ella, recogiendo su cabello en la parte superior de su cabeza. ¿Vas a venir?

Él sonrió. Estaba tratando de leer, dijo bromeando.

Está bien, dijo ella, como quieras. Y se dió la vuelta y empezó a caminar hacia el agua. Él tuvo el impulso súbito de correr detrás de ella, de empujarla al agua, o de levantarla y llevarla hacia las olas. Él imaginó cómo se sentiría su peso en sus brazos. Y entonces él puso el recibo en la página que había estado sujeta por su dedo durante toda esa sinuosa conversación, posó el libro en la toalla, y se quitó sus gafas de sol y las puso allí también, y entonces él corrió tras de ella, pero en vez de tomarla en sus brazos corrió más allá y se zambulló de cabeza en las olas delante de ella. Al pasarla, él oyó su risa, justo antes de que el agua le envolviera.

Estaba más cálida de lo que él había supuesto que podría estar. No caliente, pero no asombrosamente fría como él había esperado y las corrientes bajo las olas lo arrastraron placenteramente, ejerciendo su fuerza suavemente sobre sus brazos y piernas. Cuando él salió a la superficie, se sacudió el cabello de la cara y se secó los ojos, y casi antes de que pudiera verla venir, ella ya se estaba lanzando a él empujándolo de nuevo hacia la ola que se acercaba, hacia abajo, debajo del agua, su piel ahora muy sobre él y los brazos de ella alrededor de su cadera y el agua alrededor de ellos y él pensó en una sucesión imposiblemente rápida de pensamientos instantáneos que le hubiera gustado morir de ese modo exacto, con los brazos de ella alrededor, rodeados del agua salada y fresca, y entonces subieron para respirar, ambos jadeando, riendo, ella echando la cabeza hacia atrás en una alegría triunfante.

El agua está perfecta, dijo él.

Lo sé, podría convertirme en un pez y vivir aquí para siempre. Ella flotó hasta quedar boca arriba en la superficie y expulsó un fino chorro de agua por entre los labios fruncidos, como una pequeña fuente. El chorro describió un arco por encima de su cara y aterrizó en el agua sobre su cabeza. Él pensó en con qué facilidad ella flotaba allí. Como si fuera la beneficiaria de todas y cada una de las generosidades de la naturaleza.

Puedes ver qué halagador es que saliera de este agua para hablar contigo, dijo ella entonces.

¿Para hablar conmigo?

Sí, por supuesto.

¿Por qué?

Quería hacerlo.

¿Pero por qué?

¿Qué quieres decir con por qué? Porque quería hacerlo.

Él sonrió, y la sorprendió mirándolo de reojo desde donde estaba flotando a su lado. Ella rápidamente cerró los ojos, sonriendo con picardía cuando sus miradas se cruzaron.

Durante un rato nadaron, o flotaron, o se dejaron llevar por el vaivén de las olas, disfrutando del océano juntos en silencio. Él permaneció mayormente de pie, sumergido hasta el cuello en el agua en constante movimiento, mirando cómo salpicaba las rocas de la playa que se adentraban en el oleaje, o dejándose alzar por las olas antes de que rompiesen, mirando hacia la línea del horizonte, al océano infinito que se extendía, parecía, hasta el borde mismo de la tierra, aunque la verdad sea dicha, si ese fuera el final de la tierra esta hubiera sido muy pequeña. Él encontró este pensamiento reconfortante. Estar dentro de algo tan grande, ser sostenido tan suavemente, ser movido y dejarse mover por ello. Vio de reojo que ella estaba nadando hacia él. Los movimientos de sus brazos y piernas como una rana y una sonrisa en su cara. Y entonces ella se dió la vuelta para quedar de espaldas a él y presionó su cuerpo contra el de él, sus manos estirándose hacia atrás y adhiriéndose a él en el océano agitado. Él puso sus manos en las caderas de ella, y luego en su estómago, las puntas de sus dedos apoyadas solo suavemente en el tejido de la parte de abajo de su bañador. Sintió el hueso duro de su cadera, y sintió vagamente la topografía elevada creada por las líneas de esos tatuajes, y sintió una pizca de paz en la presión del cuerpo de ella contra el suyo. Cálida, incluso envuelta en el agua, y el olor de la sal en su cabello, que ella había soltado, y ahora llevaba sobre el hombro. Ella recostó su cabeza contra el pecho de él, la coronilla bajo sus clavículas, los brazos de él rodeándola. Creo que he decidido que eres una muy buena distracción, dijo él.

Él sintió – sí, de algún modo sintió, el pensamiento se le ocurrió – la sonrisa de ella cuando él dijo esto. Ella se acurrucó de alguna manera aún más cerca de él, quizás inclinando ligeramente sus caderas contra las de él, arqueando ligeramente su espalda para que sus hombros pudieran presionarse más completamente contra la piel mojada del pecho de él. Y quizá él presionó ligeramente sus caderas con las suyas, su mano derecha en la parte baja y plana del estómago de ella, su mano izquierda en la pelvis de ella, y él tirando de ella hacia sí. Ella subió la vista y le miró entonces, sin darse la vuelta, estiró el cuello para ver, y él bajó la mirada y la besó. O ella le besó a él, los dos besándose en el agua y las olas meciéndolos.

Se quedaron por mucho tiempo en esa cercanía, aunque su forma cambiaba aquí y allá, pero parecía como si debieran seguir tocándose. Que de algún modo se había vuelto muy importante para ambos. Y cuando salieron, fue con ella caminando delante y llevándole de la mano y ella estiró su manta sobre la arena y ellos se tumbaron juntos, uno al lado del otro, uno frente al otro, él se apoyó en un brazo, su mano superior sobre la curva de la cadera de ella, la pierna superior de ella entre las de él a la altura de la rodilla, ella recostada sobre un brazo doblado, su cabello como una almohada bajo ella. Él le apartó un mechón rebelde tras la oreja. Quizás hablaron, o quizás solamente se miraron, besándose de vez en cuando, la sal en los labios de ella, el suave calor de su lengua donde se deslizaba contra la de él. Los hombres llegaron y retiraron las sombrillas y las sillas de la playa a las cinco de la tarde y Damián y Emilia corrieron hasta las olas una vez más, su manta — sí, su manta, pensó él, la de ambos — allí sola en la amplia playa y las palmeras y otras plantas elevándose en una densa maleza detrás, y ellos dos en el agua.

La Cena

Ambos quisieron ducharse antes de ir a cenar, y entonces fueron a casa de ella y lo hicieron juntos. Ella pensó que podrían hacer el amor allí en la ducha pero más allá de tocar y besarla y muy claramente observar la forma en la que se movía, ya sin cuestionar la ética de mirarla — gracias a Dios, pensó ella — él no intentó hacerle el amor, aunque sí se excitó ligeramente mientras sus cuerpos se rozaban entre sí bajo el agua fría. Ella frotó jabón sobre la espalda de él y masajeó sus hombros y él dejó que su cabeza se apoyara delante en la piedra de la pared y ella pudo sentirle relajarse bajo sus dedos. Se besaron bajo el agua corriente, el cuerpo de ella apretado contra el suyo, las manos de él a cada lado de la cara de ella, las manos de ella en las caderas de él. Joder, te deseo, dijo él, y ella empezó a tocarle, pero él la detuvo. No, dijo él, aún no.

Tras la ducha, mientras se secaban en el diminuto baño, ella se ofreció a lavar la ropa de él y dijo que se podían tumbar mientras esperaban que se secara un poco en el tendal. Él dijo que tenía hambre y quería algo de beber, y de todos modos, su Airbnb estaba de camino a la ciudad, y ellos podrían parar allí en su camino para que él se cambiase.

Él la observó vestirse, y ella era consciente y disfrutó de los ojos de él sobre ella, mientras se aplicaba levemente su delineador y la menor cantidad posible de rímel y algo de pintalabios de aspecto natural. Ligeramente más rojo que sus labios naturales. Sutil, lo cual ella pensó que era gracioso, porque en realidad ella no se consideraba nada sutil. Mientras hacía todo eso frente al espejo, desnuda, la toalla enrollada en su cabello, poniéndose de puntillas para inclinarse hacia el espejo, ella pensó en la reticencia de él a irse a la cama con ella. O su compostura. Cuál era, ella se preguntó. ¿Era algo sobre su cuerpo, ahora que él lo había visto? Probablemente no era eso. Ella no podía evitar preguntárselo. Quizá era religioso. Quizá él solamente tenía reglas estrictas para sí mismo y ella era una tonta por pensar que solo porque era bella él las rompería por ella. Ella quería que él rompiese sus reglas por ella, pero también se entusiasmó ante la idea de que podría retarle y él no cedería. Eso la torturaba, de algún modo, que la hubiera rechazado. Aunque él no lo había hecho, ella lo sabía. Pero se sentía de ese modo, de una manera juguetona y divertida, que solo servía, para ella, para aumentar la atención, el deseo, las ganas. Una clase de poder que ahora él ejercía sobre ella.

Sí, le deseaba más por desearla y no tomarla la primera oportunidad que tuvo. ¿Cuántos hombres con los que ella había nadado habían tratado de toquetearla en el agua? Ella sentía su propio deseo y la contención de él como un pequeño dolor sordo, un calor entre sus piernas. Todo ese tiempo él estaba sentado contra el cabecero de ella, también desnudo, pero envuelto en una toalla para no humedecer la cama de ella con su bañador mientras esperaba. Él la observó todo el tiempo que ella se preparó, y ella se aseguró de mantenerse totalmente a la vista de él. Cuando terminó frente al espejo, ella dejó caer la toalla que rodeaba su cabello, dejándola en una pila en el suelo del baño, y entró caminando en su habitación, desnuda y con su cabello, aún húmedo pero ya no goteando, cayendo por su espalda. Revisó algunas prendas y tomó varios vestidos de sus perchas, pero decidió no ponérselos y los dejó también en el suelo junto al armario empotrado. Él la observó todo ese tiempo, y después de que ella revisara gran parte del armario, ella le pidió que eligiera entre un top de croché blanco roto que dejaba al descubierto la mayor parte de su abdomen, con una falda larga de color verde oliva, o un fino vestido negro que se anudaba detrás del cuello. La espalda era muy escotada, casi hasta la parte más baja de la espalda, el dobladillo llegaba hasta la mitad de su muslo, y la falda era holgada, de modo que se expandía cuando ella daba vueltas. Ella se sentía casi alarmantemente sensual en ese vestido, y escogía con cuidado las ocasiones en las que se lo ponía. En particular, le gustaba ver destellos de su reflejo en las ventanas, o los espejos, cómo se veía su espalda, expuesta, arqueada, y cómo se veían sus piernas, apareciendo bajo la falda. Ella sabía cuál quería ponerse, pero quería poner a prueba sus motivos, quizá, o quizá solo quería darle la oportunidad de participar en su vestimenta, pues ella esperaba que quizá él llegaría a sentir cierta propiedad sobre ella y que él se encargaría también de desvestirla.

Él eligió el vestido negro, lo cual la hizo muy feliz de un modo casi abrumador. Ella se lo puso para él y él se acercó detrás de ella y la ayudó a anudarlo tras su cuello – idea de ella, a pesar de que lo había hecho por sí misma, todas las otras veces – y ella se levantó, dejándole admirarla. Ella dió una vuelta y sintió la ráfaga de aire cuando la falda se levantó y sintió la emoción de llevar puesto un vestido como ese, con muy poco debajo. Ella pensó que quizá él dejaría a su mano tocar el muslo de ella durante la cena. Que quizá la tomaría con el vestido puesto cuando llegaran a casa – qué fácil sería eso. Ella podría rodear su cuello con los brazos y él podría levantarla en sus brazos y sujetarla y entonces ya no quedaría casi nada entre ellos. Ella casi se estremeció al pensarlo. Qué opinas, le preguntó, terminando de girar y colocándose frente a él.

Te ves increíblemente hermosa, dijo él, sonriendo. Parecía no estar afectado. Interesado, por supuesto, obviamente, atraído, pero no perdiendo la cabeza. Eso la inquietaba y la emocionaba. Él tomó su bañador húmedo del pomo de la puerta, donde había estado colgado, y pasó al lado de ella, besando su frente al pasar, aún envuelto en la toalla, y cerró la puerta del baño tras de sí.

Cuando él emergió un momento más tarde llevaba puesto su bañador de nuevo, y a ella le pareció de alguna manera enternecedor y simultáneamente frustrante que él se hubiera ocultado para cambiarse de nuevo a su bañador. Él la retaba de un modo que ella nunca había experimentado antes. Como si fueran antiguos amantes, como si ella fuera su chica – su chica – pero también como si tan solo fueran amigos. Ella no estaba acostumbrada a querer ser capaz de clasificar cosas. Ella prefería dejar que sucedieran como estaba destinado. Pero allí estaba, confundida, excitada, entusiasmadamente frustrada. Ella quería gritar y soltar risitas y follar. Tenía muchas ganas de follarle. ¿Nos vamos? preguntó él poniendo su mano en la parte baja de la espalda de ella. Ella asintió, y él lideró el camino desde su casa.

Cuando llegaron al apartamento de él para que se cambiara, él la invitó a entrar pero ella sintió como si debiera esperar en el salón mientras que él se vestía. Él no le preguntó qué debería ponerse. Él no revisó sus cosas para decidir qué llevar puesto. Ella no esperaba que él lo hiciera. Cuando regresó junto a ella tan solo un minuto o dos más tarde, llevaba puesto unos vaqueros bien ajustados, y una camisa blanca de lino de manga corta, y un par de sandalias de cuero. Llevaba una cadena de oro alrededor del cuello. Se veía elegante contra su piel bronceada, ligeramente enrojecida, tal vez, por la playa. Haber estado allí cuando eso sucedió la hizo sentir cálida y feliz.

Bueno, ¿No vas muy bien vestido? le dijo ella, enderezando el cuello de su camisa y desabrochando un botón más para que quedara abierta.

Él sonrió, casi tímidamente pensó ella, y se miró a sí mismo, como si se diera cuenta por primera vez de lo que se había puesto, y luego se encogió de hombros. Te ves muy guapo, dijo ella, deslizando su mano abierta por el pecho de él hasta llegar a su hombro, y entonces ella besó su mejilla. Era todo lo que podía hacer para no besar su cuello, bajo su mandíbula, tras su oreja. Para no pasar sus dedos por el cabello de él, las puntas de sus dedos acariciándole la nuca. Para no presionar su cuerpo levemente cubierto contra el de él, para no sentirle. Para no sentir su fuerza. Quién eres, pensó ella.

El restaurante al que ella había querido llevarle estaba a menos de un kilómetro. Mientras giraban desde la calle secundaria hasta una de las avenidas de la ciudad, alguien yendo en un quad saludó a Emilia mientras giraba hacia la calle secundaria de la que acababan de venir. Ella le devolvió el saludo, sonrió, y el hombre le devolvió la sonrisa y luego desapareció de su vista. Ellos continuaron caminando. Al pasar por una tienda de la esquina que vendía bikinis y otra ropa chic de playa, a las dos mujeres que estaban dentro se les iluminó el rostro al ver pasar a Emilia. Damian y ella se detuvieron, brevemente, e intercambiaron abrazos y besos en la mejilla, y Emilia les presentó a Damian y ellas intercambiaron sonrisas cómplices la una con la otra y con ella y ella les dijo que debían irse porque, por si no se habían dado cuenta, Damian estaba terriblemente desnutrido, y probablemente fallecería en cualquier momento si ella no le conseguía una bebida y algo de comer. Él les dijo amablemente que no había prisa, pero ella le acompañó a la puerta del mismo modo que un niño se escapa de una reunión social con un juguete que está entusiasmado con tener todo para sí.

Les agradas, dijo ella mientras se alejaban, tomándole de la mano y caminando ligeramente por la calle, a su lado.

¿Cómo sabes eso? ¿Dijeron eso en español y no lo entendí?

No, respondió ella, levantando la vista hacia él con timidez. Simplemente lo sé. Lo sabrías si no fuera así. Pueden ser muy buenas ocultando su aprobación, pero son horribles ocultando cuando alguien no les gusta.

Ella le miró de nuevo después de decir esto y se alegró de verle sonriendo. Él le tomó la mano el resto del camino. Ella continuó viendo gente que conocía en muchas de las tiendas, o en la calle o en quads o motocicletas. Una vieja camioneta Toyota pasó por su lado con algunos surfistas de apariencia curtida asomados por la parte trasera y todos ellos la vitorearon al pasar.

Qué, preguntó ella al notar la mirada de él sobre ella mientras doblaban una esquina.

¿Conoces a todo el mundo en esta ciudad?

Entonces ella se rió. Él parecía amar hacerla reír. No, por supuesto que no.

No te creo, dijo él.

Estoy segura de que alguien a quien aún no conozco acaba de llegar aquí. Probablemente hay algunas personas que simplemente nunca he conocido. A ti no te conocía antes de esta mañana, después de todo.

Me gusta, dijo él. Ella no pudo evitar sonreír.

A ella le daba un pequeño placer conocer al personal del restaurante al que fueron. Como si fuera algún chiste entre ellos dos que todo el mundo la reconocía. Qué familiar se sentía él ya. Ella siempre se había enamorado fácilmente, pero esto era algo distinto. Algo emocionante y peligroso.

Él intentó pedir una cerveza, pero ella intervino en español y pidió para cada uno una paloma hecha con mezcal, con tajín en el borde y una rodaja de pomelo colocada sobre el vaso.

Qué pediste para mí, preguntó él cuando el mesero se fue.

Ella no se lo dijo.

Cuando las bebidas llegaron él preguntó si también las había drogado o si solamente planeaba emborracharle.

Estoy bastante segura de que tu tamaño evitará que te emborraches antes que yo. Soy yo quien va a sufrir por culpa de mi propio entusiasmo.

¿Así que ahora me estás llamando gordo?

No, guapo, claro que no.

Él le echó una mirada especulativa. Ella batió sus pestañas en su dirección, y después se inclinó sobre la mesa y tomó la mano de él en las suyas y él se las apretó, y luego tomó un sorbo de la bebida. La saboreó, la dejó dar vueltas por su boca, y luego dijo: Sabe a combustible de barco.

¡¿Qué?! exclamó ella. ¡Combustible de barco! Ella echó la cabeza hacia atrás. Reírse era muy fácil con él. Creo que tragaste demasiada agua de mar.

¡No! dijo él, riéndose con ella. Venga, cierra los ojos y saborea el tuyo, y dime si no sabe vagamente de algún modo a combustible de barco – no el sabor real. Solo toda la sensación. Siente tu bebida, dijo él, imitando el acento de ella.

Ella cerró los ojos obedientemente y llevó el vaso a sus labios y entonces él dijo: Espera.

Él tomó el vaso de ella y lamió el tajín de un punto del borde.

¿Estás robando mi tajín? preguntó ella, con aire seriamente ofendido.

Solo confía en mí. El tajín cambia demasiado la sensación. Es demasiado potente. Solo bebe un sorbo desde este lugar, solo por este. Después puedes lamer el tajín de mi lengua si quieres.

De acuerdo, dijo ella, te tomaré la palabra. Nadie roba mi tajín.

De acuerdo, cierra los ojos como antes.

Ella lo hizo y se llevó el vaso a los labios. Olió la bebida y luego tomó un sorbo, lo hizo girar en su boca y lo tragó, y pensó que de algún modo él tenía razón. Que esta bebida que ella siempre había tomado cada vez que tenía oportunidad, ahora se había transformado, y siempre, a pesar de sus deseos o preferencias, sabría a combustible de barco. No era un mal sabor, como él había dicho, ni siquiera era una mala combinación, de alguna manera. Había algo en el aroma almizclado del mezcal y la acidez astringente del pomelo. Todo encajaba, y ella tenía que admitir que él tenía razón.

Tienes razón, dijo ella, abriendo los ojos.

¿Qué has dicho? preguntó él bromeando, inclinándose hacia delante como para oírla mejor. Se llevó una mano a la oreja. Ella se inclinó sobre la tabla y agarró la parte desabotonada de su camisa en su puño y tiró de él hacia delante con cierto cuidado, y luego dijo muy cerca de su cara, sus narices tocándose, mirándose a los ojos: Sí, tenías razón. Ahora voy a recuperar mi tajín. Y entonces ella le besó, introduciendo su lengua en la boca de él, cálida y aún con un ligero sabor a tajín, y entonces le soltó. Ella se recostó en su asiento, y se limpió las comisuras de la boca con su servilleta.

¿De dónde has salido? le preguntó él tras un momento. Se había recostado cómodamente en su silla.

De tus mejores sueños.

Tonterías.

¿Cómo, no tienes sueños?

Él no sonrió. Tengo sueños, pero ninguno de ellos se acerca ni remotamente a ti. Él tomó un sorbo y volvió a dejar el vaso sobre la mesa.

Ella se puso un mechón de cabello tras la oreja y sonrió privadamente para sí.

Ella pidió comida para ambos, todo para compartir, y en muchas de las cosas ella le dio el primer bocado, o él a ella, y ellos estuvieron de acuerdo en todo salvo en los tacos de camarones. Él insistió en que los camarones de la playa estaban mejor. Ella insistió en enseñarle a pronunciarlo correctamente. Cuando lo hizo a su satisfacción, ella brindó por su rápido progreso en español. Enseguida podrás mudarte aquí y verme. En cuanto las palabras salieron de su boca se dio cuenta de lo imprudentes que habían sido, pero ya era demasiado tarde para desdecirse y no lo hubiera hecho aunque pudiera. En respuesta a ese comentario, él simplemente dijo: No me tientes.

Después de cenar, pasearon por la playa por el equivalente de dos o tres manzanas entre los accesos a la playa, y el sol se puso en ese tiempo, como si lo hubieran planeado a la perfección, aunque no fuera así. Emilia tomó nota de este hecho y lo consideró un buen presagio de que todo parecía estar encajando perfectamente para ellos esta noche. La puesta de sol era más rica en los colores del océano que en los del cielo, pero aún así los cautivó a ambos, y por un rato se quedaron de pie allí en la playa, ella sujetando sus zapatos, él sujetando los suyos, sus pantalones vaqueros remangados por la parte de abajo, los pies descalzos de ambos en la arena, el brazo de él alrededor de la cintura de ella, descansando cómodamente en la cadera de ella, y ella con la cabeza inclinada, apoyada en el interior del hombro de él. La brisa del océano refrescó agradablemente sus pieles. Este es realmente un lugar hermoso, dijo él, y ella estuvo de acuerdo, añadiendo que parecía tener algún tipo de magia. Es algo especial, respondió él. Ella levantó la vista para mirarle una o dos veces, y, por un breve instante que ella esperaba desesperadamente recordar, le observó mientras él contemplaba el océano.

He visto este océano en varias ocasiones desde que llegué aquí. Hoy hace un rato, obviamente, pero también antes de que dejásemos la playa esta tarde, y ahora, y una vez ayer cuando llegué por primera vez. Ha sido de un color diferente cada vez.

Está muy vivo, Emilia respondió, sonriendo, con una inflexión cariñosa en su voz.

Por un rato estuvieron en silencio. El crepúsculo creció, y la playa se vació a medida que los paseantes de atardecer se iban yendo. Los sonidos de la música flamenca llegaron, difusos, desde el final de la playa. Aparte de eso y del ocasional añadido de conversaciones entrecortadas la banda sonora predominante eran las olas del océano y su incesante romper, como un suave ruido blanco ondulante, y el sonido de la brisa nocturna entre las palmeras.

No recuerdo la última vez que me sentí tan relajado, Damian dijo después de un rato.

Ella le miró entonces, él mirando el agua, y ella se giró hacia él y rodeó su cintura con sus brazos, y dejó que su cabeza se apoyara en el pecho de él. Él enredó los dedos en el cabello de ella y la abrazó ahí, y de esta forma se quedaron durante lo que parecía un momento generosamente prolongado, hasta que ella, notando la energía subiendo entre ellos de nuevo, sugirió que fueran a beber algo. Él miró su rostro, abierto y feliz, y asintió, y entonces la besó en la frente y ella casi ronroneó.

La Noche

Llegaron a un bar de tequila en la Avenida Revolución, un local decorado mayormente en color blanco con ventanas de cristal de cuerpo entero que daban a la calle empedrada y a las tiendas cerradas y al reciente crepúsculo. Escogieron una pequeña mesa en la esquina trasera, las paredes de piedra frescas incluso tras un día de sol abrasador que había horneado a la mayoría de la ciudad con su calor hasta mucho después del anochecer. Se sentaron uno al lado del otro en un reservado acolchado que se había construido en la pared, con varios cojines decorativos colocados de manera que se sentía muy natural sentarse tocándose el uno al otro. Él había escogido esa mesa, lo cual ella notó y disfrutó. Esta vez, ella le permitió pedir su propia bebida – una frase que usó en su mente, casi graciosa para ella, dado que él lo tenía claramente todo bajo control, a pesar de que esta era la ciudad de ella. Él pidió una ronda de mezcal y ella bromeó con que al parecer había quedado impresionado con el combustible de barcos. Cuando estás en México, ya sabes, respondió él. Entonces él le tocó el muslo, su gran mano cálida sobre la piel suave y tersa de su pierna.

Se tomaron las bebidas rápidamente y pidieron otra ronda, ambos pidiendo palomas esta vez. Mientras bebían y hablaban él mantuvo su mano casi constantemente sobre la pierna de ella, como si quisiera asegurarse de mantenerla cerca de él. Ella se sentía pequeña en su agarre, y excitadamente vulnerable. De vez en cuando, ella bajaba la vista y veía la mano de él sobre su muslo desnudo, tan robusta, el vello del dorso de su mano reflejando la suave luz del bar, las venas sobresaliendo de sus nudillos hasta donde su brazo desaparecía bajo la manga de su camisa. Estaría tan guapo con un anillo de boda. El pensamiento la sorprendió y ella lo alejó de su mente, sobre todo porque ella no estaba segura de tan siquiera creer en el matrimonio - de hecho había no creído en el matrimonio firmemente durante toda su vida adulta. El compromiso en general era algo que hacía que la piel se le erizase. El compromiso era para los débiles. Era para aquellos que no podían confiar en cómo eran las cosas. Era una muleta. La gente cambia demasiado a menudo como para hacer promesas para toda la vida. Volvió a mirar la mano de él ahí en su muslo y deseó que le perteneciera. No podía entender qué estaba pasando. Ella podía obligarse a sí misma a mirarle a los ojos. Pero entonces miraría sus labios.

Ella observó la avenida y asintió distraídamente a lo que él estaba diciendo. Algo sobre la energía hidroeléctrica y lo disruptiva que era realmente para lugares exactamente como este - quizá no específicamente para esta ciudad - pero cómo México como país había sufrido mucho por la mala gestión de los derechos sobre el agua en Estados Unidos. La calle se movía con gente caminando, en motocicletas, el auto ocasional - los autos parecían demasiado grandes - o camiones, y muchos, muchos carritos de golf. Una mezcla de nacionalidades. Quién se preocupa por los derechos sobre el agua, se preguntó ella. Qué concienzudo por su parte. Ella dejó que sus dedos jugaran distraídamente con el cuello de la camisa de él, con el mechón de cabello en su nuca.

No estás escuchando nada de lo que digo, o sí, preguntó él, sonriendo.

Ella le miró de vuelta, traída de nuevo al presente, puesta en evidencia. Ella casi quiso sonrojarse - quién piensa en querer sonrojarse, se preguntó - pero vio sus ojos sonrientes, su boca entreabierta, esperando por su respuesta. Él la estaba esperando. Estaba a kilómetros de distancia y la estaba esperando. Ella miró de sus ojos a su boca. Sí lo estaba, mintió a medias. Le acarició el brazo con la mano. Creo que me siento un poco borracha. Ella le hizo ojitos pero se dió cuenta incluso mientras lo hacía de que no había sido intencionado.

Él se rió fácilmente, una nueva ligereza en su comportamiento, y ella se dió cuenta de que él posiblemente también estaba un poco ebrio. No mucho. No más allá del control. Solo más suelto. Ella quería bailar con él. Ella le hizo un gesto al camarero para que les trajera la cuenta y él físicamente le impidió alargar la mano hacia su bolso cuando ella fue a pagar y ella casi soltó un jadeo, emocionada por dentro por el simple acto de agarrarle la muñeca. Su forma de sonreír mientras le decía con su cuerpo exactamente qué hacer, y qué no hacer. Y entonces deslizando un fajo de pesos dentro del vaso de cristal en el que había llegado la cuenta, él hizo una pausa, mirándolo, y después mirándola a ella.

Es típico dejar propina aquí, ¿Verdad? le preguntó él. Era tan sincero que ella casi le besó otra vez. Sí, dijo ella. Ella era consciente de estar pestañeando más veces de lo necesario. Como si la intensidad de la mirada de él la invitase a pestañear más a menudo. Y es la forma más rápida de hacer amigos, añadió, especialmente siendo turista. Ella se levantó y se inclinó y besó su mejilla mientras dijo eso último, y se detuvo un momento, oliéndole. Se dobló por la cintura para besarle, y él vio cómo el cuerpo de ella se movía en el vestido que llevaba. Vio la falda levantarse por la parte de atrás de sus muslos en el opaco reflejo iluminado de ella en el cristal de la ventana. Él quería trazar las líneas de sus tatuajes. Ven, dijo ella, vamos a bailar.

¿Bailar? dijo él sorprendido. No, yo no bailo. No soy para nada bueno bailando.

Para nada bueno bailando, se burló ella, imitando su acento. Venga. Ella tomó su mano y él le permitió ayudarle a levantarse. ¿Adónde vamos? preguntó él.

En la calle, ella se apretó desvergonzadamente contra él, agarrando los lados de su camisa en sus manos, y besó su cuello. Sígueme, dijo ella.

Ella bailó por la calle, llevándole de la mano, habiendo saludado sin mirar al camarero, a quien por supuesto conocía, y él observó el bajo dobladillo de su vestido mientras ella iba delante de él y observó cómo el cabello de ella rebotaba y sintió el frescor de la noche húmeda y olió el mar, aunque todavía débilmente, de forma sutil, como había hecho antes, y él lo inspiró profundamente por la nariz y exhaló más aire del que había inhalado en los últimos cinco años. Estaba seguro de que había gente que ella conocía cuando se marcharon, y ella le había besado así delante de ellos. Eso significaba mucho, pensó él. O eso esperaba.

Él se preguntó adónde le estaba llevando ella, pero si era sincero consigo mismo, no le importaba, y no era solo que hubiera bebido un par de copas, y no era solo que estuviera de vacaciones. Era que confiaba en ella, se dio cuenta, lo cual le parecía, sinceramente, una locura, porque ella era desde luego la persona más libre y salvaje que él había conocido jamás, menos aún de la que se había enamorado. Y entonces se dio cuenta. Se estaba enamorando de ella. Este pensamiento le hizo sonreír, porque estaba bastante seguro de que ella se estaba enamorando de él también, aunque él nunca había sido muy bueno juzgando eso, si era sincero consigo mismo. El aire era fresco sobre su piel y la mano de ella estaba fresca y eléctrica y viva y él la observó y trató de no tropezar por las calles y aceras desiguales mientras pasaban por delante de los negocios cerrados y los restaurantes que habían estado abiertos cuando habían pasado antes pero que ahora también estaban cerrados. Bajaron caminando por la Calle Marlín hasta el acceso a la playa y luego por la arena, ella aún llevándole de la mano y él yendo donde sea que ella quisiera llevarle, hasta un grupo de gente frente a una mesa de DJ con vistas a la playa. Había quizá cincuenta personas reunidas, la mayoría bailando, algunos sentados o descansando junto a pequeños fuegos que habían sido encendidos en fogatas arenosas en medio de unos bancos circulares de madera provistos de cojines. El océano se doblaba sobre sí mismo más allá en la oscuridad y él podía oírlo y olerlo y casi saborear la sal que dejaba en sus labios por la bruma que parecía cubrirlo todo. La canción que había estado sonando cuando llegaron terminó, o más bien se fundió con la siguiente, y ella tomó su mano y dio vueltas sobre sí misma y entonces se acercó a él, su cuerpo presionando contra el de él, sus caderas moviéndose con la música, sus ojos cerrados, sus manos encontrando apoyo en diferentes partes del pecho de él, o su cintura, o su cuello. O acariciando su propio cuerpo mientras ella se apretaba contra él – esto le pareció lo más érotico – y él siempre era consciente de ella, de su cuerpo, de su posición relativa a él, de sus movimientos y cómo interactuaban con él. Como si él cuestionara si ella lo deseaba. Era obvio, él lo sabía. Lo había sido todo el día. Ella le había hablado en la playa. Se había recostado contra él en las olas. Aun así él se lo preguntaba, del mismo modo que alguien cuestionaría la realidad de ganar la lotería incluso si tuviera el boleto ganador en la mano y viera los números en el panel y el confeti estuviera cayendo. Él la observó en las luces estroboscópicas y él ya no pudo enfocar sus ojos y sus pensamientos se derritieron. Ella se movió una vez más hacia él y él tocó sus caderas, o sintió la tersa piel de sus piernas, el dobladillo de su vestido cediendo a las yemas de sus dedos. Él no podía evitar moverse con ella. Era como si ya estuvieran haciendo el amor, y él se sintió casi dolorosamente excitado. Sus pensamientos se fueron. Él ya no los tenía. Le habían dejado. Era todo sentimiento. Todo sentimiento. Este era un territorio nuevo.

No se quedaron mucho tiempo en la playa, y no estuvieron mucho caminando de vuelta a su casa, parando cada treinta metros o así para besarse y tocarse el uno al otro y para reírse ante la libertad que les había habitado a ambos de repente. Se dieron prisa con la puerta, y sus labios no se separaron mientras abrían el pestillo, ni mientras ella desabotonaba su camisa ni mientras él la empujaba contra la pared, su vestido subiendo por su muslos y las manos de él sosteniéndola firmemente mientras la besaba y sus brazos rodeaban su cuello y sus piernas se abrían alrededor de él.

Ya no hablaron. Solo hicieron sus sonidos animales en la oscuridad mientras los sonidos de las olas entraban por la ventana y el viento movía las cortinas y ellos sentían la presión de la piel del otro. Se movieron como agua por la habitación. Él sosteniéndola. Ambos apretados el uno contra el otro y chocando contra las paredes, contra los muebles, su vestido tirado en una silla, ella bailando hacia atrás ante él, moviendo sus caderas sensualmente, deseando, necesitando, cayendo juntos sobre la cama. Él le gruñó – era todo lo que podía hacer. Joder, te deseo, pensó él, quizá, si sus pensamientos tuvieran palabras. Cuando él la agarró fue su piel en la de ella, y también cuando la besó en todas partes desde el arco de su pie hasta la parte de atrás de su rodilla y hasta la parte interior de su muslo y subiendo por su estómago y a lo largo de sus curvadas costillas a la luz de la luna que entraba a través de la ventana, y sus pechos y arriba y abajo por su clavícula – cuando él besó cada uno de los dedos de su mano derecha, y cuando él besó su frente, y su oreja, y la punta de su nariz, lo cual la hizo reírse con alegría, y entonces su mejilla, y el arco cóncavo bajo su barbilla, lo que la hizo jadear y arquear la espalda, y finalmente, casi desesperadamente su boca – y cuando él entró dentro de ella fue lentamente y sus miradas se cruzaron y él la miró mientras él la empujaba más allá de la realidad y ella le miró mientras los ojos de él se voltearon involuntariamente ante la absorbente presencia del cuerpo de ella alrededor de él. Sus frentes se encontraron, agarrándose al mundo tangible, con una necesidad energética de saber que estaban allí, juntos. Estoy aquí, él le dijo a ella. Y yo también, ella le respondió. No con palabras. Con contacto.

Al principio lo que ella había sentido era la intensidad de su presencia. El compromiso que él exudaba, con el momento, con ella, consigo mismo. Eso era una elección consciente, ella lo sabía. Él se lo había mostrado cada vez que podría haberla tenido y había decidido no tomarla. Esto es lo que quiero, le dijo él con su cuerpo. Pero ella le sintió contenerse, también. Por cortesía. Por respeto a ella, a su cuerpo, a las reglas en las que aún creía. Y entonces ella le besó subiendo por su cuello, y ella mordió su oreja, con fuerza.

En el calor del instinto él agarró su cuello y la apretó contra la cama. Él la miró, una llama en sus ojos, su mano alrededor del cuello de ella, y ella le devolvió la mirada con una intensidad aún mayor. Como una invitación. Un reto. Tómame. Había una antigua conversación silenciosa entre sus ojos en ese momento. Algún gran entendimiento, la complejidad del respeto y la degradación desarrollada en el teatro sexual en el curso de un instante. Y él, viendo la emoción en sus ojos, la abofeteó, aunque él no sabía por qué. Un destello de conciencia temporal. Una pregunta. ¿Está bien? Sí, me gusta. Dámelo. Más fuerte. Fóllame. Te necesito.

Él agarró un puñado de su cabello y la giró sobre su estómago, y ella se arqueó desesperadamente hacia él, agarrando puñados de sábanas con ambas manos, suplicándole con cada insinuación física que tenía disponible que la tomara completamente. Y él lo hizo. Él presionó dentro de ella tan profundamente que ella se sintió a sí misma desmoronándose. Era casi más de lo que podía soportar, pero él susurró en su oído en ese preciso momento que ella se sentía tan increíble y ella sintió el calor y la intensidad de su excitación y ello la ablandó con él, de tal modo que ella habría muerto en su manos si él hubiera querido. Tómame, ella suspiró. Fóllame, por favor. Sí – era una súplica. Era todo lo que ella había necesitado alguna vez. La manera en la que el océano la sacó, la empujó hacia dentro y hacia abajo. Cómo una tormenta le arrancó la decisión de vivir o morir. Era el poder de la ola. En ese momento él era la tierra y ella era la luna e incluso mientras ella le prestaba la fuerza de su gravedad él aún se movía por voluntad propia, y ella le seguía. Ella sacaba lo mejor de él, pero ella le seguía, siempre. Y entonces él se estaba viniendo, y ella le sintió profundamente dentro de ella y ella se sintió a sí misma contraerse contra él, y así ellos murieron juntos, solo por un momento, de la misma manera que una persona muere bajo el agua cuando hay fuerzas jugando más allá de la capacidad de comprensión humana.

Joder, lo siento, dijo él. Él jadeó contra su cuello, su pecho contra su espalda, ambos acostados por completo en la cama, excepto por las caderas de ella, las cuales aún se movían animalísticamente hacia él. Ella se rió, pero no podía hablar. Aún estaba ahogándose en él, y sus manos ni siquiera estaban alrededor de su cuello ahora. Él besó su sienes y su mano encontró la parte baja de la cintura de ella y se aferró a ella, él aún en su interior, y él exhaló pesadamente ante ella, y entonces él colapsó encima de ella.

El peso de él era inmenso. Era más que la suma de su masa física. Eres un animal, le dijo ella, sintiéndole aplastarla, casi asfixiada agradablemente. Nunca había hecho eso antes, dijo él. Ni siquiera sé de dónde vino eso.

Estaba en ti, dijo ella. Yo solo lo saqué.

Si tú lo dices, dijo él. ¿Estuvo bien? ¿No te hice daño?

No, dijo ella suavemente, placenteramente exhausta. Me encantó. Fue perfecto.

De acuerdo, dijo él. Él movió su peso, sintiendo que debería dejar algo de espacio para ella bajo él. No se apartó. Solo cambió su postura de manera que su peso recayera más en sus brazos y sus piernas y menos completamente en el cuerpo de ella, el cual se sentía tan pequeño bajo el suyo. Él inspiró profundamente el olor de ella, el olor de ambos, aún dentro de ella, aún envuelto en su calidez, y ella envuelta en todo su cuerpo. Eso es lo que es, pensó ella. Estamos dentro el uno del otro. Como respirándonos el uno al otro, sin barreras entre nosotros. Qué lujo. Él se había rendido al efecto que ella tenía sobre él, y fue entonces cuando él dijo que la amaba.

Ella se rió en voz alta. Shhh, dijo ella, sonriendo felizmente. No hables. Pero él ya lo había dicho, y hablaba en serio. Y a ella le había gustado por una fracción de un instante, al menos. Lo siento, dijo él entonces. Yo solo...

Shhh, dijo ella de nuevo, amablemente, suavemente, tranquilizándole. Ella pasó sus dedos por su cabello, alargando la mano hacia atrás, atrayéndole hacia sí aunque él estaba encima de ella y ella estaba boca abajo en la cama. Ella se dio la vuelta, él saliendo de ella, ella sintiéndole derramarse fuera de ella sobre la cama. Ellos estaban en un lado de la cama, podían dormir en el otro. Está bien, dijo ella. Ven aquí. Ella le abrazó. Él bajó por su cuerpo de modo que su cabeza podía apoyarse en su pecho y ella podía abrazarle bien. Sus brazos envolvieron la cintura de ella. La parte estrecha de su cintura. La parte que un corset hubiera asfixiado. Y aún así sus brazos no eran asfixiantes. Dejaban espacio para que ella respirara. Como si no hubiera hecho él eso siempre. Todo el día, pensó ella, y se rió. Siempre, hoy. Cuál era la diferencia. Él la abrazaba y la dejaba respirar. Águilas volando juntas, aire más que suficiente para ambas, alas fuertes y capaces, el viento soplando a su alrededor, y libertad. ¿Y no era eso lo que ella siempre había querido? Estar sostenida y ser libre al mismo tiempo. Ella exhaló pesadamente, pasó sus dedos por su cabello. Él sintió el subir y bajar del pecho de ella. Él se hundió en ella. Él se durmió instantáneamente en el espacio creado por su rendición. Y ella también.

El Amanecer

Él escuchó a los gallos primero, y se preguntó por la hora en la oscuridad. Él miró de reojo a un lado por entre la presión sorda en su cabeza y encontró a Emilia durmiendo, de cara a él, recostada de forma entrañable. Incluso al dormir ella era caótica, ¿Y qué encontraba él digno de amar en eso? Solamente todo. Mientras él la observaba dormir, él mismo solamente medio despierto, él tuvo el sentimiento de que algo estaba empezando. Él volvió a caer en un sueño poco después. Un sueño de agua, de olas, de sol. Sin tierra a la vista, solo el océano por kilómetros en todas direcciones, y sin miedo, tampoco. Solo el océano. Solo el océano.

Cuando él se despertó mientras el sol finalmente entraba por las ventanas, no fue la luz lo que le despertó en realidad, sino el cuerpo de ella acercándose al suyo, su espalda contra la de él, ella de lado y de espaldas, pero buscándole. Él se giró, puso su brazo bajo su cabeza. Su brazo superior la rodeó y ella entrelazó sus dedos con los de él y se apretó más contra él. Ella tal vez estaba aún dormida. Y él quizá también. Quién podía decirlo en esa tenue luz del amanecer. Ella presionó su cuerpo desnudo contra él de nuevo de ese modo que sugería que ella sentía que ellos no podrían - nunca - estar lo suficientemente cerca para satisfacer su necesidad de tocarle. Él se puso duro, y ella presionó contra él de nuevo. Pequeños movimientos adormilados, de parte de ambos, y algo ardiente, cálido y vivo entre ellos. Ella se estiró hacia atrás y le introdujo en su interior, ambos quietos por un momento en su unión. Y entonces hicieron el amor lentamente, adormilados, sus cuerpos meciéndose eternamente en el espacio entre la oscuridad de la noche y el resplandor de la mañana. Ellos se quedaron dormidos en esa posición exacta y él no se despertó de nuevo hasta media mañana. Ella ya había estado despierta por algún tiempo cuando él abrió sus ojos y fue bajo su mirada que él recuperó la conciencia. Ella estaba recostada allí, con la cabeza apoyada en una mano, su cabello cubriéndole medio rostro, su cuerpo al descubierto y la habitación cálida y quieta. Cuando él la vio, él sonrió, y ella también sonrió. Un momento suspendido. Cuántos momentos de quietud hacen una vida, se preguntó él. Para ella era entrañable y mágico cómo el amor podía en realidad parar el tiempo. ¿Era esto? pensó ella. Era esto amor. Oh, a quién le importa cómo se llame. Él la observó, y ella se permitió ser observada. ¿Dormiste? preguntó ella.

Él asintió, pero no contestó. Bien, dijo ella. Ella le besó y entonces ella salió de la cama.

Fue demasiado pronto, su alejamiento. A él le hubiera gustado que ella se subiera encima de él. Que le tomase en su boca, quizá. O que tan solo se quedase recostada en su pecho por un momento más. Cada instante sin tocarla ya era doloroso. Jesucristo, pensó él. Qué estás haciéndote a ti mismo.

Ella se había puesto un par de pantalones cortos que apenas cubrían nada y recogiendo su cabello en la parte superior de su cabeza, de pie junto a la cama, dándole la espalda. Él la observó pasivamente. Ella miró sobre su hombro y le preguntó qué estaba mirando. A ti, dijo él. Bien, respondió ella. Eso es lo que esperaba. ¿Tienes hambre? ¿Quieres desayunar? ¿Café? ¿Té?

Eres una persona mañanera, a que sí, dijo él.

¡Por supuesto! dijo ella. Y nocturna. Soy una persona de cualquier hora del día. ¿No te gustan las mañanas?

Él gruñó y se hundió en la almohada. Ella se rió y él tuvo que esconder su sonrisa. Joder, pensó él. Sí que estoy acabado.

Ella hizo café y le llevó un poco a él a la cama, y él se sentó y sostuvo la taza humeante con ambas manos.

Mira cómo la luz se refleja en el vapor, dijo ella, sentándose en la cama a su lado. ¿No es muy bello?

Tú eres muy bella, dijo él y tomó un sorbo, el cual estaba aún demasiado caliente y él lo sabía, pero necesitaba hacer algo con su boca antes de decir nada más. Necesitaba quemar la estupidez de su lengua, quizá. Ella besó su hombro.

Tengo una clase de yoga en media hora, dijo ella. Eres bienvenido a quedarte aquí si quieres. Volveré después de la clase. ¿Quizá podríamos dar un paseo hasta la playa para nadar?

Él cambió su mirada de la superficie negra y similar a un espejo del café a su rostro, tan brillante, tan feliz. Me gustaría eso, dijo él. Bien, respondió ella. Eso es lo que quería que dijeras.

Hey, sobre anoche. No usamos protección y yo—

Está bien, dijo ella sonriendo y poniendo su mano, aún cálida por la taza, en el antebrazo de él. Tomo la píldora. No es problema, de verdad. Te hubiera detenido. También es mi responsabilidad, ya sabes.

No, no lo es realmente – debería haber usado un condón.

Shh, dijo ella. Está bien, Damian. Me encantó. Me encantó por completo. Fue perfecto.

Ella le miró a los ojos mientras dijo esto y su expresión era tan sincera y tan amable y tan indulgente. De acuerdo, respondió él. Aun así, lo siento.

No lo hagas, dijo ella. Yo no lo siento.

De acuerdo, entonces yo tampoco lo siento.

Bien.

Además, sobre lo que dije al final...

¿Qué, que me amas?

Sí, eso, dijo él mirando al techo y sonriendo a pesar de sí mismo, suspirando y rindiéndose al reconocimiento de su propia metedura de pata.

Bueno, ¿Lo dijiste en serio?

Obviamente sí que quería decirlo. Aún quiero. Aun así, probablemente debería haber tenido más autocon—

No, si lo dijiste en serio, hiciste bien en decirlo. Su determinación en esta afirmación era absoluta.

Pero te hizo sentirte incómoda, ¿No?

¿A mí? No – sorprendida, quizá. No lo esperaba, pero no me incomodó.

Él asintió.

Creo que a veces somos demasiado cuidadosos con nuestras palabras, cuando el whole point de ellas es expresar lo que vive dentro de nosotros y compartirlo con el mundo, o con aquellos que amamos.

Pero las palabras pueden herir a la gente. Mucho, a veces.

Bueno, sí, por supuesto. Eso no es lo que quiero decir. Quizá me estoy explicando mal. Yo solo digo que, especialmente cuando se trata de hacer cumplidos a la gente o demostrar nuestro amor o ser honestos sobre algo que estamos sintiendo, creo que esas cosas necesitan decirse. Por ejemplo, puedo decirte que anoche en el bar pensé que tu mano podría verse muy bien en un anillo de boda. Yo quise que fuera la mano del hombre que me perteneciera. Nunca antes había querido eso realmente, al menos no desde que soy adulta. Siempre he estado muy en contra del matrimonio o de cualquier tipo de compromiso para toda la vida porque quién sabe qué querrá en dos años o en veinte. Pero lo sentí anoche. Quién sabe lo que significa. Probablemente no significa nada – solo que lo sentí.

Él estaba observando el vapor que se elevaba de su taza y escuchando sus palabras y dentro de él había una calidez que él nunca había sentido, al menos conscientemente. Quizá como un niño. Aunque quizá ni siquiera entonces.

Pero esa es otra cosa, a que sí, ella continuó. Deberíamos hablar libremente, creo, pero también permitirnos el uno al otro decir lo que sentimos en el momento y no tomarnos el uno al otro demasiado en serio. Es decir, me amas ahora, me amaste anoche. Quizá yo también te amo. Pero cambiará. Eso era entonces, esto es ahora, y lo que vendrá, vendrá, porque por supuesto que las cosas cambiarán, ¿O no? Por supuesto que sí, y cuando cambian tenemos que ser libres para insuflar vida al cambio, también. No debería ser tan malo decir que amas a alguien, o que has pensado en casarte con esa persona, y aún entonces darte espacio para darte cuenta que tal vez era una intensidad pasajera que solo necesitaba ser expresada.

Él estaba frunciendo el ceño ahora, no necesariamente en desacuerdo, sino pensando, quizá incluso en diálogo consigo mismo de algún modo, sobre lo que ella estaba diciendo. No estoy seguro de eso, dijo él. Siento que nuestras palabras son una de las cosas que podemos darnos el uno al otro que significan algo. Si no puedes confiar en la palabra de alguien, ¿Cómo puedes confiar en ellos? Haría que sus palabras tuvieran muy poco significado.

No estoy de acuerdo – yo diría que si alguien no puede ser honesto sobre los cambios en su corazón, ¿Cómo puedes confiar en ellos?

Él pensó en esto. Tenía que ser ambos, pensó él. Ser honesto, y ser cuidadoso con las palabras. Creo, dijo él tras un momento, que eso es importante, por supuesto, decir la verdad de lo que estas sintiendo. Solo creo que es responsabilidad de cada persona no expresar cada impulso pasajero, y obviamente yo no cumplí eso demasiado bien anoche.

Está bien, dijo ella. Soy muy sexy y estabas perdido en mí. Ella lo dijo como si fuera una verdad irrefutable.

Él se rió entonces, encantado con su fácil sentido del humor incluso en medio de una conversación seria – un desacuerdo, incluso. Sí, de acuerdo, lo dejaré pasar. Cómo puede ser tan segura de sí misma, pensó él. Y por su parte, ella era consciente de estar siendo muy arrogante en ese momento, pero era todo parte del juego. ¿Por qué no? Era muy divertido.

Veo lo que estás diciendo, de todos modos, dijo ella tras un momento. De verdad. Y respecto a ese punto, creo que a veces lo que creemos que es examinar cuidadosamente lo que decimos antes de que lo digamos – a veces estamos solo intentando pulir algo difícil de decir. ¿Sabes? ¿Es esa la frase correcta? Casi como una forma de manipular. Escoger las palabras con demasiado cuidado se siente casi como engañar, ¿O no?

Yo no lo creo así. Pero también veo lo que quieres decir. Por supuesto, alguna gente manipula su forma de decir algo para hacerlo sonar de cierto modo. Como las mentiras por omisión, por ejemplo.

Sí, exactamente. Eso es exactamente lo que quiero decir. Ella lanzó sus manos al aire en acuerdo. Su rostro era tan amplio y feliz. Y otras cosas, dijo ella, pero ese es un muy buen ejemplo. Ella miró el reloj en el microondas y se levantó. Tengo que prepararme para salir, dijo ella. Pero no puedo esperar a seguir con esta conversación más tarde. Ella pasó su mano por la nuca de él y a lo largo de su hombro y entonces entró al baño.

Él se reclinó contra el cabecero de la cama, la taza de café ahora vacía sostenida holgadamente en sus manos, y cerró los ojos. Él podía oír los sonidos de la ciudad, los grandes camiones de agua que retumbaban ruidosamente por la ciudad, demasiado grandes para las calles, pero aceptados con una especie de tolerancia amistosa y respeto mutuo. Él escuchó a los gallos cantar sin cesar desde todas las partes de la ciudad, lo cual era confuso, pensó él, porque ya era por la mañana. Él llegaría a saber que ellos cantaban sin importarles la hora del día o de la noche y que nadie realmente les prestaba ninguna atención. Él escuchó a los pericos en los árboles de afuera parloteando, las voces de gente paseando y hablando los unos con los otros en español y él captó unas pocas palabras aquí y allá, pero en su mayoría no entendía nada. Él escuchó el sonido del lavabo del baño corriendo de forma intermitente, en pequeñas ráfagas, y los sonidos de la puerta del armario del baño abriéndose y cerrándose, los productos colocándose en la encimera de concreto. Él juró que también podía oír la luz del sol. Y el océano, aunque estaba demasiado lejos para poder escucharlo realmente durante el día. Lo escuchó todo quizá, todo el mundo en alguna vaga y resonante canción en el viento. Él inspiró profundamente. Ella apagó la luz del baño. ¿Estarás aquí cuando vuelva? preguntó ella. Él abrió sus ojos, la miró, asintió y sonrió. Salvo que vengan a por mí, dijo él.

Ella besó su frente. Espero que esperen hasta que vuelva para que pueda besarte de nuevo una vez más antes de que ellos se te lleven.

Les pediré que esperen antes de llevarme, dijo él. Por ti. Disfruta de tu clase.

Ella sonrió, sus labios contra los de él. Mi amor, dijo ella. Gracias, disfruta de la mañana.

Te amo, dijo él. Ella tocó su mejilla y le sonrió. Ten cuidado, dijo ella, con la fina línea entre el amor y la posesión. Y solamente dilo cuando sea amor.

¿De dónde has salido? Él le preguntó.

De tus mejores sueños, dijo ella. He venido a rescatarte.

Or destrozarme.

Bueno, lo uno o lo otro, dijo ella. Y entonces se fue.

El Día

Cuando ella se fue, él puso su taza en la mesilla de noche y se tumbó en la cama de nuevo, empujando las sábanas hasta su cintura, entrelazando sus dedos bajo la almohada debajo de su cabeza. El ventilador de techo movió el aire sobre su piel desnuda y él agradeció en silencio a quien sea que hubiera inventado los ventiladores de techo. Pensó que quizá se quedaría dormido pero en cambio él miró fijamente las vigas del techo y los ladrillos cóncavos que se arqueaban entre ellos, las marcas de quemaduras de su cocción, el mortero de color crema entre ellos, las sombras del sol que se filtraban a través de las cortinas.

Y ella había salido por la puerta, su esterilla de yoga colgada al hombro con su correa tejida, un regalo de un amigo en su último cumpleaños, y ella había pasado su pierna por encima de su motocicleta y accionado el embrague y presionado el arranque con su pulgar y lo había sentido petardear momentáneamente y luego ronronear con suavidad entre sus piernas. Ella giró la motocicleta y empezó a bajar por la calle. Ella amaba la sensación del viento en su cabello y le encantaba cómo las calles empedradas hacían vibrar a la motocicleta mientras ella conducía. El sol era brillante y caluroso y el día era interminablemente húmedo y ella sentía el sudor en su frente incluso mientras conducía, pero no le desagradaba el calor. Así disfrutaba aún más del viento, pensó ella. Bendito viento. Bendito sol.

Desde la cama él dejó que su mente vagara en una especie de plácido deambular por el recuerdo de lo que había sucedido durante las últimas veinticuatro horas y lo que iba a suceder en las próximas cuarenta y ocho. Él se había enamorado. Es esa la correcta palabra para ello, se preguntó él. O la frase correcta. Fue ilógicamente rápido, pero su atracción también fue ilógicamente fuerte. Además, esto era lo que se hacía – quizá no de vacaciones en otro país y quizá no en el transcurso de un día, pero enamorarse era uno de los hitos de la vida, seguido de casarse y tener hijos, o no, pero en cualquier caso el amor tenía que estar allí en algún punto, y quién era él para decidir cómo esas cosas llegaban a suceder. Él se frotó los ojos y se preguntó si había más café.

Ella condujo por la ciudad hacia la gran colina en el margen exterior de la Avenida Revolución y ella sintió la bruma saliendo de la rueda delantera de la motocicleta por las calles húmedas que en algunos lugares solo habían sido lavadas, y ella vio las tiendas abriendo y a algunos de los restaurantes abrir con sus sillas y mesas puestas en la calle. La gente que ella conocía la saludó y ella sonrió y también les saludó. Ella pasó de nuevo por la tienda de ropa que sus amigas tenían y vio a María llegar justo en ese momento y subir la persiana de metal y ella la saludó y continuó. El sol era brillante y claro y el cielo libre de nubes por completo. La ciudad tenía un olor fresco, el viento soplaba generosamente desde el oeste ese día en vez de desde el sur, y estaba trayendo el aroma del océano. Ella se topó con un auto parado en la carretera, con las luces de emergencia encendidas, la puerta trasera abierta y alguien descargando cajas en un quiosco cerrado, y ella lo rodeó, deslizándose entre otra motocicleta que se acercaba y el auto parado y luego otro peatón, y sintió el latido de su habilidad como un pedazo de orgullo en su pecho.

Había más café, y él lo echó en su taza, aunque ya no estaba ardiendo. Él pensó en meterlo en el microondas, pero decidió beberlo solo cálido. Él miró la cama pero sintió que era momento de mover sus piernas un poco. Así que él caminó por la pequeña casa y casi distraídamente miró sus cosas. Había pequeños tesoros por todas partes. Pequeñas figuras de arcilla, conchas marinas, cristales, un mazo de tarot, un incensario con cenizas en pequeños grumos cilíndricos debajo del palito que estaba medio quemado en el soporte. Él miró sin ver los libros en su estantería, la mayoría en español, pero algunos en inglés. Un par, en realidad, en francés. Puede hablar francés, se preguntó él. ¿Y ahora? Sus pensamientos continuaron. ¿Y ahora qué, viejo? Vuelas a casa en dos días. Mañana por la noche, en realidad. ¿Y entonces qué? Ella no se va a ir. Fue hecha para este lugar, o ello para ella. O lo que sea - no se irá a ningún lado. Y tú no se lo pedirías de todos modos. ¿Cómo va a cambiar esto por una casa de estilo artesanal en un camino de tierra en el bosque de Idaho? Bueno, tenemos aguas termales, él se imaginó a sí mismo diciéndole, medio en broma. No, ella no se va a mudar. ¿Y tú? Qué, vas a cancelar tu vuelo. O mejor aún, solo piérdelo. Eso sería jocosamente despreocupado por tu parte, ¿No? Casi se rió en voz alta ante este pensamiento. Solo no aparezcas, se dijo a sí mismo. Sí, eso es.

Ella iba subiendo por la gran colina, pasando por la construcción de los nuevos apartamentos, donde los obreros mezclaban cemento a mano y clavaban clavos en sus encofrados de madera, gastados por el uso, que se moldeaban una y otra vez para construir más casas de las que nadie podría contar. Las tablas utilizadas en la construcción de casas, igual que los obreros, eran anónimas para los futuros habitantes, pero indispensables para el mundo. Ellos desaparecieron de su vista enseguida cuando ella dirigió su atención a los reductores de velocidad y se metió por el estrecho hueco que había en medio de la calle, girando a la derecha de nuevo para dejar espacio para dejar espacio a un carrito de golf que iba en dirección contraria. La pequeña niña en el carrito y su madre, sentada al lado, la miraron y sonrieron y en realidad la saludaron, y Emilia les sonrió de vuelta y les guiñó el ojo y entonces ellas también se fueron. Ella bajó por el otro lado de la colina y giró hacia Punta de Mita y poco después estacionó la motocicleta a la sombra del gran árbol en frente del estudio. Caballete abajo, la motocicleta cálida bajo sus piernas desnudas, ella pasó su pierna por encima mientras Aditi la llamaba desde el umbral de la puerta, dándole la bienvenida.

Él sacó un disco de una caja de leche, Jackson Browne Remastered, y lo puso en el tocadiscos. Entonces lo volvió a tomar, sopló un poco de polvo que tenía en la parte superior y lo volvió a dejar en su sitio. Pensó en subir al avión, en subir al avión solo. Nunca vas a olvidarla, pensó él. Ella literalmente te perseguirá para siempre. Qué más da, quédate. Pierde el vuelo, o cancélalo si eso te ayuda a dormir mejor. Mejor aún, solo cambia la fecha. Quédate unos pocos días más. Quédate una semana. Llama al trabajo y diles que tienes disentería. O giardia. Lo que sea que puedas pillar aquí. No pienses en eso, te enfermarás. Había empezado el segundo lado del disco sin querer realmente y mientras él nadaba en ese mar de pensamientos sobre qué diablos iba a hacer, el estribillo llegó y las armonías en realidad le hicieron detenerse. Había algo especial en la música, la luz y el olor del café. Las sábanas de la cama, la hendidura de su cuerpo aún de algún modo donde ella había dormido, su forma aún en la almohada. Él aún podía verla allí en la penumbra de la madrugada, la forma en la que su cabello cubría su rostro e incluso todavía podía ver que ella estaba sonriendo. Quién sonríe mientras duerme. Quizá sería más feliz aquí pensó él. Había más paz en esta pequeña ración de la que él había conocido en toda su vida anterior.

Ella se acercó saltando a Aditi y le dio un abrazo, sonriendo ampliamente. Alguien está feliz hoy, dijo su amiga. No solo feliz, ¡Estás brillando! Parece que hayas sido follada como se debe.

¡Aditi! dijo ella, fingiendo ofenderse. ¡No hables de ello de ese modo!

Bueno, ¿Qué se supone que diga?

No sé, ¿Algo un poco... más dulce?

Pero lo has sido, a que sí...

Ella apartó la mirada, observando la calle brillante, mirando los autos y camiones pasar, sonriendo para sí. Cuando ella miró de nuevo a la mujer en la puerta, le brillaban sus ojos. Ella asintió.

Qué bueno, me alegro – bueno, trae toda esa hermosa y efímera buena energía a clase. Necesitarás una correa y dos bloques salvo que te estés sintiendo extra flexible hoy.

Eres demasiado, dijo Emilia, apretando su hombro al pasar.

Él revisó sus emails archivados en su celular y encontró la confirmación de su vuelo, y entonces se desplazó hasta la parte inferior, donde aparecía el número de teléfono del servicio de atención al cliente. Él tocó el número y le apareció la ventana para iniciar la llamada. Él presionó el botón lateral en el celular y la pantalla se fue a negro. Ella probablemente ni siquiera quiere que te quedes, pensó él. Sí, pero entonces por qué ella me pediría que me quedara en su casa mientras ella estaba fuera. Quién confía en un extraño así, solo en su casa. Ella probablemente hace esto a menudo, en realidad. Ella probablemente devora turistas. El pensamiento le hizo reírse. Como si ella fuera alguna clase pequeña, bellísima mujer carnívora sexualmente desviada que saciaba su necesidad de sexo salvaje con hombres del estado de las patatas que conocía en la playa. El afecto que él sentía por su caos era estimulante, en realidad. La deseaba de nuevo. Él se preguntó cuánto tiempo pasaría antes de que ella regresara. Él calculó la duración de una clase promedio de una hora, cuándo ella se fue, cuánto tiempo le tomaría llegar allí, y volver. Se preguntó, también, si ella pararía en algún sitio. Quizá ella en realidad quería que él se fuera mientras ella estaba en la clase. Esa sería una manera muy limpia y digna de hacerlo. Dejarle la puerta abierta, pero la opción de quedarse. De quedarse más de lo necesario, ambos habiendo expresado sus intenciones positivas, y ambos alejándose en silencio, manteniendo intacta la dignidad de todo el mundo. ¿Pero no acababa de pregonar ella esta misma mañana la importancia de las palabras sinceras? Ella no habría manipulado la situación así. Él tomó un sorbo del café y se dio cuenta de que estaba mejor ahora que no estaba quemando. Él podía saborearlo de verdad, incluso a pesar de la quemadura en la punta de su lengua de antes. O quizá ella le había quemado cuando él la besó. Mujer diabólica. Él sonrió.

La clase fue dura, y ella sudó copiosamente, usando una toalla aquí y allí para limpiar los charcos de su esterilla para no resbalarse en ella en las distintas posturas de equilibrio. Ella disfrutaba del reto, el impulso dentro de ella de aguantar una respiración más, una respiración más, una respiración más. Y entonces la dulce liberación. A ella le encantaba cómo se sentía sentirse fuerte. Sentirse capaz. Allí estaba de nuevo, sentirse capaz. Y entonces ella pensó en él, y cómo ella disfrutaba de que él la dirigiera. No porque él pensara que ella no pudiera – o porque él necesitara el control. En la química entre ellos se asumía que él tenía el control y que ella le seguiría felizmente. Parezco un cachorro indefenso cuando él está alrededor, pensó ella. Uttana Shishosana – cachorro extendido, Aditi anunció. Vete de mi mente, Emilia pensó, sonriendo. Y por qué tienes que usar palabras sánscritas. Siempre le había molestado. Una especie de superioridad de los instructores de yoga. Qué tontería por la que preocuparse, pensó ella. Pero no era preocupación de verdad. Era como el pensamiento de la preocupación – como si fuera una parte de una versión diferente de sí misma y en este espacio mental, en esta forma de ser en este día particular, no le molestaba en absoluto. Era como si ella pudiera verlo y reírse amablemente ante la frivolidad de todo salvo el amor.

Cuando ella volvió a casa él estaba sentado en una silla cerca de la ventana de la cocina, leyendo un libro que ella reconoció como uno de los suyos. Era El Alquimista. Una versión ilustrada, con ilustraciones de Moebius, el artista francés. A ella le encantaba ese libro, y le encantaba que él lo hubiera encontrado y elegido. Él levantó la vista ante el sonido de la puerta y sonrió al verla, y entonces se levantó para ayudarla con las cosas que ella traía.

Hola, guapo, dijo ella, poniéndose de puntillas para besar su mejilla. ¿Tienes hambre?

No estoy famélico, dijo él.

Mmm, dijo ella felizmente. Me gusta esa palabra. Bueno, pasé por la panadería francesa y compré algo de pan para nosotros en caso de que tuvieras hambre. Huélelo, ella le ordenó, y abrió la bolsa de papel marrón sosteniéndola lo suficientemente arriba para que el aroma se escapara hacia él. Él se inclinó, lo olió, y entonces dijo: De acuerdo, ahora sí tengo hambre. Bien, dijo ella. Ahora tenemos la respuesta correcta. Ella le dio la bolsa y le preguntó si él podría cortar el pan.

Tú pareces tener un talento especial para leer todos mis libros favoritos, dijo ella desde la otra habitación mientras ella colocaba su esterilla de yoga en la esquina.

¿Sí? preguntó él desde la cocina. Él estaba cortando la baguette y un poco de queso que ella le había dicho que sacara del refrigerador, y poniendo pequeños conjuntos de los dos en un plato. Ella volvió y puso su mano en la parte baja de la espalda de él, aún desnuda, aunque él se había puesto sus vaqueros en algún momento. Ella se inclinó hacia su hombro con sus labios. Ella le olió. Hueles bien, dijo ella.

Él la miró. ¿A qué huelo?

Mmm, a ti. Nada que pudiera nombrar. Quizá tan solo un poquito como yo. Es solo un buen olor.

Estaba preocupado de que olería mal dado que no me he duchado esta mañana.

Ella negó con la cabeza, sus labios aún contra su piel.

Supongo que estos van juntos, dijo él señalando con el cuchillo al queso y el pan que él estaba cortando. Ella asintió, aún sin quitar sus labios de su hombro. Oh, dijo ella de repente. Esto también. Ella tomó un gran tomate y lo puso junto a la tabla de cortar. Voy a cambiarme, añadió ella. Estoy horriblemente sudada.

Necesitas ayuda, preguntó él sobre su hombro. No esperaba una respuesta, mucho menos una favorable. De hecho, tan pronto como lo había dicho él se había arrepentido.

Si tú quieres, dijo ella insinuante. Él miró sobre su hombro de nuevo a tiempo de verla desaparecer al girar la esquina hacia su habitación mientras ella estaba sacando su top por su cabeza. Él hizo una pausa, posó el cuchillo, y la siguió.

Cuando él giró la esquina hacia la habitación, ella estaba esperándole, aún en sus shorts, y cuando él entró ella le saltó encima e inmediatamente comenzó a besarle. Me estás arruinando para cualquiera, dijo él a través de sus besos. Ella colocó su dedo índice contra sus labios y dijo shhh. Oh, tú shhh, dijo él. Él la tumbó en la cama y bajó sus shorts por sus caderas y entonces él besó hacia abajo por el centro de su estómago tan lentamente que casi le hizo sentir dolor por dentro. Cuando él besó entre sus piernas, ella estaba ya muy mojada, y ella sintió el músculo de su lengua hacer contacto con sus partes más sensibles con una sensación casi abrumadora. Él tenía sus manos en el exterior de sus muslos, en la parte superior donde ellos se juntaban con sus caderas, y él estaba sujetándola en la cama y en sus manos había el sentimiento de que ella no iba a irse a ningún lado hasta que él la hubiera reducido a nada salvo sentimientos y quizá algún ruego a Dios. Ella ya estaba muy cerca de ese final nirvánico y ella pasó sus dedos por el cabello de él mientras él hacía cosas con su boca que ella nunca había experimentado. Ella gritó, jadeando, en el aire tranquilo de media mañana. Él gimió de ella cuando él la sintió venirse, y entonces él besó el interior de sus muslos y la baja curva de su estómago bajo su ombligo y él mordió suavemente la piel tensa sobre la elevación de su pelvis y él pasó una mano sobre el pecho de ella y entonces como si él no fuese un hombre maduro ella tiró de él hasta que quedó encima de ella como una manta y él descansó una vez más en su pecho y ella acarició la sombra de barba en su mandíbula y ella pasó sus pequeños dedos delicados tras la oreja de él y ella tiró del lóbulo de su oreja y ella peinó sus cejas y ella besó su coronilla y entonces exhaló mil años de soledad.

Qué demonios, dijo ella, era eso. Ella le sintió sonreír contra sí. ¿Eres una chica feliz? preguntó él. Una chica muy feliz, respondió ella. Bien. Él besó su esternón y entonces se relajó en sus brazos. ¿Cómo aprendiste a hacer eso?

En realidad no aprendí, por así decirlo.

Bueno, claramente sabes lo que haces.

Hmm, dijo él tras un momento. Solo estoy haciendo lo que se siente correcto. En realidad no he estado con mucha gente.

¿Cuánta?

¡No puedes preguntar eso! dijo él mirándola.

Acabo de hacerlo. He estado con veinticinco hombres.

Él la miró, y entonces besó el centro de su pecho.

Y diecisiete mujeres, añadió ella.

Él se rió y era el tipo de risa en la que incluso él no estaba seguro si ella estaba bromeando o hablando muy en serio y en cualquier caso a él realmente no le importaba. Qué esperar de una mujer tan bella. El número era en realidad menor de lo que él hubiera pensado, pero él no lo dijo.

Y tú, preguntó ella hacia su cabello, como lo preguntara directamente de su cabeza.

Muchas menos, respondió él.

¿Cuánta? No soy tu primera vez, ciertamente.

Ha, no, dijo él. No eres mi primera vez. Qué, pensabas que era virgen o algo. No, no eres mi primera vez.

Diez, entonces, dijo ella.

Menos, respondió él.

¿Cinco?

Él sacudió su cabeza contra su pecho donde ella le abrazó.

Bueno, dímelo, entonces.

Él la miró, la miró a los ojos, y sonrió. Ella era muy buena.

Eres mi cuarta, dijo él. Eso es probablemente vergonzoso, a que sí.

¿De verdad? Preguntó ella. Él podía sentir que ella había levantado su cabeza para mirarle.

De verdad verdadera.

Creo que eso es muy admirable, en realidad, dijo ella tras un momento, apoyando su cabeza hacia atrás en la cama. Y para ser sincera me hace sentir muy especial.

Qué estamos haciendo, preguntó él entonces.

Justo ahora estamos tumbados juntos, y entonces comeremos, y luego iremos a dar un paseo. Ella estaba haciendo pequeños dibujos suaves con sus uñas en la espalda de él.

¿Y tras eso?

¿Quién sabe? ¿Quizá nadar? O cenar algo. Quizá me harás el amor de nuevo.

¿Y mañana, y el día siguiente?

Ella se rió fácilmente. Quién sabe lo que mañana traerá de todos modos. ¿Estás preocupado por ello? Tenemos ahora mismo, después de todo. El momento más importante de todos.

Él asintió y no preguntó nada más, y ella pudo sentir algo en él retraerse.

Aunque ojalá cada día pudiera ser así de maravilloso. Y habiendo dicho esto ella cerró los ojos y ella pudo sentir algo elevarse de nuevo dentro de él, y en ese momento ella se preguntó si la luna alguna vez tenía miedo del poder que tenía sobre el mar.

La Tormenta

En el calor de pleno mediodía, ellos caminaron juntos de nuevo por la ciudad a su apartamento y entonces fueron a un quiosco a por una botella de vino y luego hasta la playa. Ellos tomaron un camino que ella quería mostrarle, que pasaba por la jungla en vez de ir por la carretera con todos los resorts y restaurantes turísticos. El camino subía abruptamente y cuando ella le miró en los escalones esperando verle bastante detrás y esforzándose por mantener el ritmo, él estaba justo detrás de ella y ni siquiera parecía que él estuviera respirando con dificultad.

Mister fit, bromeó ella. Es la altitud, dijo él. Donde vivo está a más de 6,000 pies sobre el nivel del mar. Eso es qué, ¿Casi 2,000 metros? El aire aquí lo hace fácil para mí. Ah, claro, claro, dijo ella, ella misma casi sin aliento. Está bien – aquí estoy yo pensando que te he ganado con esta pequeña caminata y tú no estás ni siquiera esforzándote. En este momento, impresionada por su fuerza, por el reto de la colina, ella se emocionó también por el hecho de que su fuerza hubiera superado a la suya. ¿Estás mirando mi trasero mientras caminamos?

No soy un animal, respondió él.

Ella miró hacia atrás sobre su hombro, con picardía. Claro que sí, lo he visto. Un simple hombre no hace el amor así.

Él se rió jovialmente. Me haces algo, dijo él.

Y entonces ella paró y se dió la vuelta para mirarle. ¿Estás pasando un buen rato? preguntó ella con increíble sinceridad.

Claro que sí, dijo él. ¿Por qué?

Porque hay tristeza en tus ojos.

Él hizo una pausa, mirando las vistas. Ellos podían ver el océano desde este mirador. Él observó las olas romper sobre las rocas en la base de la colina y observó más allá cómo las pequeñas motas de gente subían y bajaban con las ondulaciones perpetuas del océano. Bueno, dijo él, si soy honesto ya estoy preguntándome cómo voy a seguir adelante con mi vida tras dejarte.

Ella dio unos pocos pasos hasta él, ella cuesta arriba y casi a su misma altura en el camino, y puso sus brazos alrededor de su cuello y le miró. Él le devolvió la mirada con firmeza. Él no sentía tanto pánico diciendo esto como él había esperado. En realidad, él no había esperado decirlo en absoluto, pero habiéndolo dicho él era consciente de estar anticipando ya sea una respuesta evasiva, o su incomodidad, o algo más desconocido pero realmente desfavorable. Sé lo que quieres decir, dijo ella.

No parece que te moleste en absoluto.

Ella le sonrió muy dulcemente. Bueno, solo estoy intentando disfrutar el tiempo que tenemos juntos.

Él asintió.

Ven, dijo ella. Estamos casi allí. Podemos hablar más en la playa, o mejor aún, en el agua. Me estoy quemando. El océano lo arreglará todo.

Ella le besó y entonces volvió a su lugar ante él y él se encontró a sí mismo miserablemente dividido entre la esperanza, la desesperación y la rendición.

En la playa, la misma playa, un poco más de veinticuatro horas después de que ella se había sentado a su lado, ambos en el mismo punto. Nuestro sitio, había dicho ella. Qué cruel asumir la posesión de algo en nombre de ambos cuando la realidad del hecho era que esta era la playa de ella y él estaba solo de visita, y cuando él se fuera, él volvería a casa como un hombre totalmente diferente, y su corazón nunca la dejaría de verdad, y ella probablemente seguiría con su vida como si nada hubiera pasado. Él sonrió a medias y posó la bolsa que había llevado. Se quitó la camisa y dijo que quería nadar.

Bueno, por supuesto, dijo ella, sonriendo. Eso es para lo que hemos venido, después de todo. Mientras decía esto, ella estaba bajándose los pantalones cortos y quitándose la ropa que cubría su cuerpo, y algo en los ágiles movimientos de su cuerpo bronceado le ablandó. Cuando ella estuvo lista, él la observó leer la expresión en su rostro. Ella dio un paso hacia él y tomó su rostro en sus manos. Hey, dijo ella. El agua ayudará.

Cómo podría, pensó él. Cómo podría. No podría, por supuesto. Porque el agua no puede cancelar vuelos, salvo quizá el clima si cuentas eso, o los tsunamis, o las inundaciones, o qué demonios. Estás arruinando esto para ambos, pensó él. Detente. Él cerró sus ojos e inspiró, y pudo sintió la sal en su nariz, y por primera vez, de algún modo, desde que ellos habían llegado a la playa, él escuchó las olas. Él sonrió involuntariamente. Abrió sus ojos, y entonces se separó de ella y corrió tan rápido como pudo hacia las olas, y pudo escucharla riendo alegremente detrás de él, y entonces él sintió el agua rodear sus pies y luego sus piernas y las olas rompiendo contra sus rodillas y la perfecta temperatura del agua y la arena volviéndose grava brevemente bajo sus pies mientras él corría, y entonces la arena volviendo, la topografía irregular de las corrientes, y entonces él pisó un agujero y se cayó de cabeza al agua cuando una ola llegó, y el agua salada llenó su nariz y él cerró sus ojos y cuando él salió a la superficie el día era brillante y perfecto, y ella estaba allí a su lado riendo y echándose el cabello hacia atrás.

Eres un hombre salvaje, dijo ella, aún riendo.

Él la miró, y miró alrededor. Al agua extendiéndose hasta el horizonte, a las colinas descendiendo hasta el océano, cubiertas de árboles y verdes contra el cielo despejado. Él vio, allá en la orilla, a dos niños jugando en la arena, enterrándose el uno al otro y soltando risas. Tenías razón, dijo él.

¿Oh? Preguntó ella.

El océano hace que todo sea mejor.

¿Ves? dijo ella, con una amplia sonrisa. Te lo dije. Ella le salpicó y él nadó hacia ella, sus brazos agarrando la cintura de ella y ambos cayendo en las olas.

Ellos nadaron como lo habían hecho el día anterior, un baile espontáneo de contacto y separación, de individualidad y unidad. El océano era un medio entre ellos, un perfecto ecualizador, una fuerza mística de la naturaleza, del amor, del ser. En él ellos eran perfectos, y el sentimiento se quedó con ellos tanto tiempo como las últimas gotas de ese agua permanecieron en sus pieles.

En la playa, ellos se durmieron y se despertaron ante alguien preguntando si ellos harían una donación a una organización que manejaba orfanatos. Él era un hombre muy mayor, vestido con una camisa blanca abotonada y vaqueros, y un sombrero de cowboy de estilo del oeste. Él estaba afeitado y llevaba botas, y él llevaba una hebilla de cinturón de rodeo.

Él les contó la historia de una niña que se había estado quedando con su abuela mientras sus padres emigraban a los Estados Unidos para encontrar trabajo. Ellos fueron detenidos por las autoridades de inmigración varias semanas después y estaban siendo retenidos. Y entonces la abuela se había enfermado y había muerto, y la niña había caminado 60 kilómetros hasta la estación de autobuses más cercana y habló con alguien allí que pidió ayuda y el orfanato había sido contactado, y ella aún estaba allí, esperando la liberación de sus padres como si eso pudiera pasar, pero por lo demás sola. Damian escuchó la historia atentamente y cuando hubo terminado él le dió al hombre todos los pesos que tenía en su billetera y le preguntó por una web o una dirección donde él pudiera donar más de lo que llevaba encima en ese momento. El hombre estrechó su mano enfáticamente y le llamó un buen hombre y estrechó su mano de nuevo y le dijo, en inglés, que Dios estaría con él. Entonces el hombre descendió por la playa.

Damian se sentó un rato después de que el hombre se fue y miró al mar. Cuando Emilia se sentó y pasó su mano por su espalda y le preguntó si estaba bien él asintió. Creo que esa historia me afectó de verdad, dijo él.

Ella estaba en silencio pero continuó tocándole. Entonces ella dijo: No sé si esa historia era cierta. Pero hay un montón de historias reales así.

Él asintió, sin hablar.

Realmente pone nuestros problemas en perspectiva, dijo él tras un rato.

Sí. ¿Aún tienes a ambos padres?

Él asintió. ¿Y tú? preguntó él en español.

Ahh, ¡Muy bien! ella se alegró. Entonces su rostro cambió, y ella dijo que había perdido a su madre cuando era adolescente. En sus ojos estaban la resignación y la rendición de alguien que ha trabajado duro para superar algo muy trágico. Él había visto esa mirada antes. No en ella, sino en otra gente. Una especie de sinceridad triste, desconocida excepto para aquellos que la habían sentido.

Lo siento, dijo él. ¿Qué edad tenías?

Dieciséis, dijo ella, sonriendo ahora. Ella era una mujer asombrosa. Mi héroe. Y ahora, mi mártir.

¿Tu martyr? Él se preguntó si esta era una palabra que ella no entendía del todo en inglés.

Una gaviota aterrizó en la playa ante ellos y ambos la miraron brevemente. El viento sopló con más fuerza y la gaviota alzó el vuelo y se fue.

Sí, por supuesto, dijo ella, sonriendo de nuevo. Cuando ella murió descubrí en mí esta nueva libertad de convertirme en lo que sea que quisiera. Ella murió por mi causa, creo. No como si yo fuera responsable de su muerte o nada de eso, o como si ella tuviera que morir para liberarme. Todo eso suena muy dramático cuando lo explico de ese modo. No, más bien que porque ella vivió tan poco tiempo, siento que mi responsabilidad como hija es vivir por ella. Vivir lo que ella no pudo vivir.

Mientras escuchaba, él recordó lo que ella le había dicho sobre mudarse, vivir en diferentes países. Él pensó en todo lo que ella le había dicho sobre su visión del compromiso y del amor y de la honestidad y de darle palabras a lo que sea que surja en tu corazón y entonces él lo entendió.

Creo que esa es una manera muy bella de verlo, dijo él cambiando su mirada desde el mar a ella.

Ella sonrió dulcemente. Gracias, dijo ella. Bésame.

Y él lo hizo, y ellos se tumbaron una vez más en la toalla y no durmieron sino que se recostaron cada uno con sus ojos cerrados y escucharon los sonidos de la playa. Los vendedores les dejaron solos y la brisa sopló placenteramente y él sintió el sol en su piel y la arena donde se había secado en él y él sintió la piel de ella, también, y el subir y bajar de su aliento. Él se preguntó si ella se mudaría a Idaho. Quién era él para decidir su próximo capítulo. Parecía que incluso ella no poseía completamente esa habilidad. Entonces él se sentó y dijo, Creo que voy a quedarme un poco más.

Ella estaba tumbada sobre su estómago ahora, su cabeza girada hacia él, y abrió los ojos. ¿En la playa? preguntó ella.

No, dijo él poniéndose de costado para mirarla. Aquí. En Sayulita.

Ella cerró los ojos de nuevo, aún sonriendo. Creo que has estado bebiendo agua de océano de nuevo.

Algo en su pecho se encogió. No, dijo él. Lo digo en serio. Estoy muy feliz aquí. Y tienes razón, la vida es muy corta. No puedo imaginarme dejando este lugar cuando me siento tan bien aquí. No aún, de todos modos. Y tú, pensó él. No puedo obligarme a dejarte. Pero él no lo dijo.

Ella se dio la vuelta y se sentó y pasó sus dedos por su cabello. Damian, dijo ella. Sé cómo te sientes.

¿Pero? preguntó él.

Ella suspiró. Veo lo que sucede.

¿Qué quieres decir?

Ella hizo una pausa, o dudó, u organizó sus pensamientos. Él no estaba seguro exactamente de qué estaba pasando en su mente, salvo que él sentía como si ella estuviera formulando un plan de escape y el nudo en su pecho se apretó. Así era como siempre iba a ser, pensó él.

No es sobre ti, dijo él antes de que ella pudiera hablar. Quiero decir que me alegro de haberte conocido, obviamente, pero de verdad siento que este es un lugar en el que me gustaría pasar más tiempo.

Ella se rió. Por supuesto que es sobre mí, dijo ella. Dentro de ella había surgido un sentimiento tan intenso de estar atrapada que ella no podía explicarlo. ¿No había ella misma pensado en su mano con un anillo de boda justo la noche anterior? ¿No se había sentido ella más a salvo con él que en cualquier otro momento en su vida, especialmente con cualquier otro hombre? No lo sé, Damian. Yo solo – tienes una vida entera en Idaho y yo quiero que te quedes aquí, pero no puedes quedarte para siempre. Lo sabes, y yo lo sé.

Y qué, ¿Sientes que como no puede ser para siempre no merecen la pena unos pocos días más?

No, no es eso. Pues, sí, quizá lo es.

Él se sentó y se inclinó hacia delante en sus rodillas. Ella se levantó ligeramente y se impulsó a sí misma en sus codos.

Él estaba limpiando la arena de sus tobillos. Dijiste ayer que debería mudarme aquí y entonces yo podría verte siempre que quisiera.

Sí, dijo ella, tocando su mano, deteniendo sus rápidos movimientos. Quizá. Y lo decía en serio entonces. Todavía hablo en serio. Era un sueño – una fantasía – sería algo bello.

¡Entonces por qué estás diciendo que no debería quedarme? Él alejó su mano de ella y acercó más sus rodillas a su pecho con sus brazos.

Porque no se supone que sea de ese modo, dijo ella tras un momento, silenciosamente.

Él esperó a que ella continuara, pero ella no lo hizo. ¿Qué quieres decir, Emilia, con que no se supone que sea de ese modo?

Pues... No puedo decirlo de ninguna otra forma. Es solo lo que es. Tú no estás destinado a quedarte aquí y yo no estoy destinada a mudarme a los Estados Unidos (cómo había sabido que estaba pensando esto, se preguntó él), y nosotros somos solo una estrella en el cielo – un brillante punto de luz, y entonces ardemos. Y está bien, porque es bello mientras dura.

Él se frotó la frente con ambas manos con exasperación. Entonces él miró la brillante y clara línea del horizonte.

Pero quiero que dure más.

Le impactó cuando dijo esto que podían haber sido las palabras más honestas y vulnerables que él nunca había pronunciado.

Ella se arrimó a él en la manta y besó su hombro. Yo también, dijo ella.

Entonces qué estamos haciendo, preguntó él.

Estamos peleando cuando solo tenemos un poquito más de tiempo juntos, le dijo ella a su piel. Así era como se sentía. Como si ella estuviera hablándole a su piel, a su cuerpo, a las partes de él que sabían sin saber. Al animal. Al pequeño niño que entraba corriendo en el océano libremente, salvaje. Al hombre que aún debía emerger pero que estaba dentro, en algún lugar, esperando a ser despertado por completo.

La declaración detuvo sus pensamientos. Él se detuvo, cognitivamente paralizado, y de algún modo el nudo que había estado en su pecho, ya aflojado por el cuerpo de ella al lado del suyo, ahora tan cerca, se aflojó por completo gracias a sus palabras.

Él asintió. Lo siento, dijo.

Yo también.

Él giró su cabeza hacia ella y ella le besó y entonces ella le preguntó si le gustaría nadar una vez más antes de que volvieran caminando a casa. Él quería preguntar si podía quedarse con ella esa noche, pero él no se lo preguntó. Y ella sintió la pregunta en la punta de la lengua mientras se levantaba y sacudía la arena de sus piernas, y ella le sonrió por no preguntar. Pero si él hubiera preguntado, pensó ella, ella habría dicho que sí, aunque ella sintió ganas de decir que probablemente sería mejor si ellos no lo hicieran. Y al no preguntar, él había alquimizado de algún modo su sentimiento de encierro y obligación y culpa, y en vez de eso había abierto la puerta a que ella decidiera por sí misma lo que ella quería, y en ese espacio ella se dio cuenta de que de hecho ella había esperado que él durmiera a su lado por una noche más.

Si él pudiera seguir siendo este hombre. El hombre seguro de sí mismo, confiado. El hombre que la amaba sin necesidad de sostenerla demasiado fuerte. El hombre que confiaba en ella. Eso era lo que era, realmente. Confianza. Ella necesitaba que él confiara en ella y la dejara ir, y supiera que, como un pájaro, ella siempre volvería. Soy como un pájaro, pensó ella. Qué fácil se rompen mis huesos.

Ellos nadaron juntos de nuevo pero esta vez mayormente no se tocaron, y él no se acercó a ella, ni la siguió, ni pareció necesitarla cerca en absoluto, y al mismo tiempo él no parecía estar haciéndolo por despecho. Era más como que él estaba en su propio mundo, pensativo, reflexivo, presente consigo mismo y con el momento. A ella le gustaba eso. Le miró secretamente. Como había hecho el día anterior, antes de ir a hablar con él. Ella se hundió bajo el agua cuando una ola llegó, y se quedó bajo el agua tanto tiempo como sus pulmones se lo permitieron, escuchando la ola rompiendo sobre su cabeza, las corrientes bajo ella y cómo el agua revolvía la arena en el fondo del océano, sintiendo la luz y su resplandor refractado bajo la superficie del agua. Ella sintió la quietud causada por la ausencia de aliento, y se preguntó si en el momento antes de la muerte, después de que el corazón se parara, podía encontrarse una quietud similar. Era casi un placer cesar de estar viva. La increíble paz. Una paz inexplicable, pensó ella. Cuando subió a la superficie, él estaba flotando boca arriba y ella nadó hasta él y pasó sus dedos por su cabello bajo el agua y acercó su cabeza a su pecho y se inclinó hacia adelante y besó su frente. Él sonrió sin abrir los ojos.

Estás listo, preguntó ella mientras él se ponía de pie y secaba el agua de su rostro. Él abrió los ojos y la vio allí en el agua, brillante, dorada bajo el sol, la luz que el agua reflejaba bailando por su rostro.

Él la besó una vez más en la boca, y entonces se separó de ella y le dijo, Sí.

Ellos caminaron desde la playa casi en silencio. Llegado un momento, ella dijo, Gracias. Él preguntó por qué, y ella le dijo: Por compartir tus sentimientos conmigo. Él casi dijo: Siento haberme emocionado. Él casi dijo: Siento haber arruinado nuestra tarde. Él casi dijo: Gracias. Finalmente, él no dijo nada, y ellos siguieron caminando.

Cuando llegaron a la habitación de él, él dijo que iba a ducharse y leer un rato y le preguntó a ella si le gustaría ir a cenar o a tomar una copa con él en unas pocas horas. Ella casi le invitó a hacer esas cosas en su casa, y sintió algún instantáneo aunque efímero pánico ante el pensamiento de separarse de él, pero no le preguntó. Ella le dijo que viniera a recogerla cuando estuviera listo. Él asintió, y la besó, y entró a su habitación y cerró la puerta.

Mientras ella se alejaba, le echaba de menos. Saboreaba, en realidad, el sentimiento de echarle de menos. Qué regalo le había hecho él. Añorarle. Quemaba como un dolor en su pecho, y ella lo saboreó. Añorar a alguien es saber que les amas. Fue lo que su primer novio le había dicho cuando la dejó ir. Ella no lo entendió entonces – solamente sabía que ella debía irse y estaba segura mientras se iba de que ella estaba arruinándolo todo a costa de sus propias convicciones para vivir la vida que estaba destinada a vivir – pero él había dicho eso y ella se había dado cuenta de que él tenía razón y ella le había amado tanto por ello, porque él le había dado en esa simple frase la paz que la ayudaría a sobrellevar los siguientes meses difíciles. Cuánto le había enseñado él, realmente, sobre la vida y el amor. Qué buen hombre había sido. He conocido a tantos buenos hombres, pensó ella.

Tras cerrar la puerta, él se quitó sus shorts y se fue inmediatamente a la ducha. Y allí se quedó hasta que el agua se enfrió, y entonces se mantuvo allí hasta que algo dentro de él decidió que era momento de salir. Quién podía decir cuánto tiempo estuvo bajo el agua. Era egoísta, él lo sabía. En este lugar donde el agua era tan escasa y costosa. Pero lo necesitaba. Él pensó en el orfanato. Necesidad – qué variados los significados de esa palabra. Él no necesitaba estar en la ducha. Un niño necesitaba a sus padres. Y él tenía a los suyos, y esos niños probablemente nunca tendrían a los suyos. Dios, este mundo, pensó.

Una vez se hubo secado, buscó el nombre del orfanato que el hombre en la playa había dicho. Él no podía recordar el nombre exacto, pero buscó organizaciones regionales y encontró una que parecía familiar. Estaban localizados en el sur, casi en Puerto Vallarta, y él pasó algún tiempo aprendiendo lo que pudo por internet, aunque no pudo localizar una página web. Por un momento durante este tiempo él había considerado el relativo anonimato del mundo en desarrollo, especialmente comparado con los Estados Unidos. Cómo en sus círculos sería impensable para una organización reputada no tener una página web. Y cómo la sociedad continuaba funcionando aquí en ausencia de tantas infraestructuras supuestamente necesarias, tanto como lo había hecho antes de la llegada del internet. La gente llevaba sus mensajes con ellos, la historia se preservaba en las historias contadas alrededor de la mesa a la hora de la cena, los celulares se usaban más para la comunicación inmediata y táctica que para nada más. Por supuesto, ellos aún tenían redes sociales aquí. Él había visto a niños viendo vídeos breves en un celular fuera de unas pocas de las tiendas, y se había preguntado qué tipos de cosas había en el lado español del internet, comparado al lado anglosajón. En este momento le impactó lo grande que era el mundo realmente y lo muy poco que él conocía en realidad.

Mientras ella caminaba junto a uno de los bares, alguien que la conocía llamó su atención. Ella se había detenido a decir hola, había terminado sentada, y en ese momento estaba bebiendo una cerveza.

El chisme es que tienes un novio, dijo Yusuf. Él era un antiguo amigo suyo que se había mudado a Sayulita más o menos al mismo tiempo que ella, él también hablando varios idiomas, habiéndose mudado primero desde una ciudad en las afueras de Mumbai, y habiendo vivido después en la República Checa, luego en Madrid, y ahora habiéndose mudado a México. Él siempre había trabajado en el turismo, pero decía que prefería trabajar en bares porque así se aprende más sobre el mundo. Aprendí eso en Praga, dijo él.

Tú y tus chismes, dijo ella. Ellos hablaban a menudo en inglés para que él pudiera practicar, y porque él decía que hacía que los turistas americanos estuvieran más dispuestos a entrar si la charla era en un idioma que ellos entendían.

Bueno, ¿Es cierto? preguntó él.

Por qué estás tan interesado, preguntó ella. Tienes un crush en mí o algo.

¿Un crush? Preguntó él. No conozco esa palabra. Crush.

Significa que sientes amor por mí, dijo ella sonriendo y tomando un sorbo de su cerveza.

Por supuesto que sí, pero eso no es lo que importa aquí.

¿Y eso sería? preguntó ella.

Bueno, ¿Es cierto que tienes un nuevo novio? preguntó él de nuevo. Toma, take some tequila. Te hará hablar conmigo.

Se dice have some tequila, en inglés.

Como sea, have some tequila, dijo él sirviendo dos chupitos.

No lo sé, dijo ella. Creo que voy a verle esta noche y no sé si me apetece beber aún.

Ah, quieres estar completamente presente para tu amor. Él pronunciaba sus erres enfáticamente.

Shhh, dijo ella, y tomó el chupito. Sí, si debes saberlo, conocí a un hombre ayer y salí con él anoche.

¡Ah! exclamó él, dando una palmada en la barra. ¡Lo sabía!

Cállate la boca, dijo ella, aunque ella sonrió mientras lo dijo, y observó la calle. Se estaba fresco en el bar con los ventiladores encendidos aunque todavía era un día muy caluroso.

Pues, ¿Cómo se llama ese hombre?

Se llama Damian. Pero creo que es difícil para él conocer a alguien de vacaciones.

Qué quieres decir, preguntó Yusuf. ¿A él no le gusta entregarse, o...?

Ja, ella se rió. No, lo contrario. Él quiere quedarse, y amarme para siempre.

Ah, bueno, no puedes culparle, respondió él. Cómo no amarte.

Mi amor, dijo ella, cariñosamente. Sí que tienes un crush en mí.

Sí, por supuesto. ¿Te gusta él tanto así? ¿O quizá no?

Sí que me gusta, dijo ella, deslizando sus dedos por la condensación en su botella de cerveza. Me gusta mucho.

Bueno, quizá sean esos miedos que vuelven para atraparte.

Qué miedos, preguntó ella, sonriendo de nuevo.

Oh ya sabes, ¿No sucedió esto mismo con ese hombre en Indonesia? ¿Del que dijiste que estabas tan enamorada? ¿Y tú solo tuviste que irte, como dices?

Cállate, dijo ella. Entonces ella hizo una pausa. Sí, quizá fue algo así.

Verás, creo que ese quizá es que tienes un poquito de miedo del compromiso. ¿Cuál es la palabra? ¿Commitment? Ella asintió. Sí, que quizá no estás tan segura de ti misma o piensas que te frenará de alguna manera.

Yo no tengo miedo del compromiso.

Bueno, entonces estás muy comprometida con tu libertad. Lo cual no es tan malo, excepto porque eventualmente quizá te sentirás sola.

Esto es cierto, dijo ella. ¿Puedo tomar otra cerveza?

Por supuesto, dijo él sacando una del refrigerador y abriéndola por ella. Dame la botella.

Ella intercambió botellas con él y soltó un exasperado suspiro. Por supuesto que tengo miedo del compromiso, dijo ella. Lo sé. No sé por qué lo niego. Si pudieras oír mi diálogo interno, lo sabrías. ¿Es mejor o peor, saber todo lo que sucede dentro de ti?

Yusuf se rió genuinamente. Sí, mejor por supuesto, dijo él. Puedes imaginar no saberlo. Sería como volar un avión sin ver.

Volar a ciegas, dijo ella, es el dicho.

Sí, bueno, como sea, dijo él. Al menos tú puedes verlo.

Pero aún controla lo que hago. Es como que puedo ver el sentimiento venir pero no puedo hacer nada para detenerlo.

Eso es muy natural, creo.

Él dijo hoy que quiere quedarse más tiempo y yo le dije todo tipo de razones por las que él no podría, pero en realidad creo que solo entré en pánico y pensé, y si él se queda y tenemos una vida muy feliz juntos pero él se odia a sí mismo – y me odia a mí – en cinco años porque rompemos, porque a veces gente lo hace, y entonces todo es mi culpa por arruinar su vida perfectamente feliz.

Yusuf pensó por un momento, asintiendo, bebiendo una cerveza. ¿Crees que él tiene una vida muy feliz?

No lo sé – él parece un poco uptight, realmente.

No conozco esta palabra. Uptight.

Como estresado, dijo ella.

Ah, bueno. Bueno, y dijiste que él es un hombre, ¿Sí?

¿Quieres decir, no una mujer?

No, respondió él riendo. Quiero decir que no es un chico. Mi punto es si él es lo suficientemente mayor como para tomar sus propias decisiones.

Ella le miró por un largo rato. Eso creo.

Creo que te importan mucho los demás, y quieres que todos sean felices. Creo que tienes miedo de no hacer lo correcto, y hacer daño a la gente. Pero creo que a veces tú haces más daño a la gente porque actúas por miedo.

Ella le miró por un largo rato otra vez. Un camión de agua pasó ruidosamente por la calle de afuera con tanta fuerza que habría sido imposible escuchar su respuesta de todos modos. Ella esperó. El camión pasó. ¿Y qué crees que debería hacer? preguntó ella.

Me alegro de que me lo hayas preguntado, dijo él. No lo sé.

Eres de mucha ayuda.

Bueno, yo nunca afirmé poder solucionar tus problemas, chica, yo solo te pregunto cuáles son.

Qué útil, dijo ella, poniendo los ojos en blanco.

Hey, dijo él. Es mi chisme.

Debería irme, dijo ella. Necesito ducharme y creo que él probablemente vendrá a mi casa en breve para recogerme para la cena.

Por supuesto. ¿Qué vas a decirle?

Ella exhaló un suspiro entre sus labios. No lo sé. Creo que solo voy a sentirlo y ver qué dice él.

De acuerdo, ve a hacer lo que sientes. Siente a este hombre que amas tanto. Dale muchos besos y dile que quieres que sea feliz.

¡Ay, cabrón!

Tú viniste aquí por voluntad propia, recuerda.

Y cada vez me pregunto por qué lo hago.

Buena suerte, chica, le gritó él mientras ella se alejaba.

Damian cerró su computadora y vio que la luz estaba desapareciendo rápidamente afuera. El sol se había transformado en atardecer, aunque aún no se había puesto. Él miró la hora en su celular. 6:30 pm. Él deslizó el dedo por la pantalla, pulsó unos pocos iconos y el celular empezó a sonar.

Hey, hermano, dijo una voz en el otro extremo.

Hey, ¿Te molesto?

Nunca. Solo estoy cocinando algo de cenar para los niños. ¿Qué pasa? ¿Cómo van tus vacaciones tropicales?

Van bien. Me encanta estar aquí.

Wow, ¿Te encanta estar allí? En realidad no pensé que tú dirías eso.

¿Por qué no?

Porque es un país en desarrollo y te gustan los sistemas que funcionan.

Los sistemas sí funcionan aquí. Son solo... sistemas diferentes. Supongo.

¿Has estado alguna vez en México?

No, excepto cuando éramos niños y solíamos visitar Juárez con la familia.

Deberías venir alguna vez. Tráete a los niños. Las playas aquí son increíbles.

Estás al norte de Puerto Vallarta, ¿Verdad?

Sí.

Quizá algún día. Pero son demasiado pequeños ahora mismo para disfrutarlo.

De acuerdo. ¿Cómo están, por cierto?

Oh, astutos como siempre. Everett se cagó en los pantalones y entonces se echó las cortinas encima.

Ah, ¿Escondiéndose detrás de ellas de nuevo, supongo?

Sí, no sé por qué hace eso.

No durará mucho.

Espero que tengas razón.

Yo siempre tengo razón.

Entonces, ¿Has conocido a alguna chica, o has estado solo en tu habitación?

Veo que tienes muy buena opinión de mis habilidades sociales.

Esa no es una respuesta.

En realidad sí que conocí a alguien.

Hay un silencio en la línea. El sonido de agua corriendo al fondo. Un llanto infantil. Entonces la voz dice: Espera un segundo.

Damian puede oír a su hermano llamando a su esposa para que le ayude a calmar el llanto. Entonces Damian pregunta, ¿Es esa Esther?

Sí, ¿Cómo lo has sabido?

Ella hace ese grito cuando llora. No creo haber oído a Everett hacer eso.

Ya aprenderá. Dale tiempo. Okay, espera, ¿Qué? ¿De verdad conociste a alguien?

Sí, ¿Es tan difícil de creer?

No, por supuesto que no. Solo te estoy poniendo las cosas difíciles. ¿Quién es ella?

Su nombre es Emilia. Ella vive aquí.

Ahh, ¡Una chica local!

No es de aquí originalmente. Ha vivido en un montón de lugares. En realidad no sé de dónde es originalmente. Quizá Francia o algo así.

¿Y habla inglés?

Muy bien, en realidad. Y español. Ella parece conocer a todo el mundo en esta ciudad.

Ella parece lo opuesto a ti.

No tienes ni idea.

¿Qué?

Ella es solo un espíritu muy libre.

Qué bien que estás probando cosas nuevas.

Bueno, el problema es que creo que me enamoré de ella.

Es solo el cerebro en modo vacaciones. No estás enamorado de ella, solo estás enamorado del sentimiento que tienes ahora mismo y no quieres volver a la realidad.

¿Pero cómo sabes que esto no es la realidad? Estoy viviéndolo, después de todo. Cómo podría no ser realidad.

Bueno, pero no puedes vivir en la playa para siempre. Tienes un trabajo aquí que no puedes hacer allí. Y no hablas el idioma. Y es un país extranjero. ¿Cómo podrías tan siquiera mudarte allí?

Podría, probablemente. Podría hacer mi trabajo en remoto hasta cierto punto. No tendría que trabajar tanto dado que vivir es mucho más barato aquí. Y podría aprender el idioma.

Estás pensando en ello de verdad.

Sí, supongo que sí. Realmente no me había dado cuenta de que había pensado en ello.

Una pausa.

Bueno, se te oye feliz. Relajado.

Lo estoy, hombre. Me siento realmente bien aquí. No sé si lo dije antes.

Lo hiciste. O yo lo sentí, no lo sé.

Una pausa.

Bueno, tu vuelo despega mañana por la noche, ¿Verdad? Qué vas a hacer.

No tengo idea. La cuestión es que le planteé la idea de quedarme unos días más y ella como que se asustó bastante.

¿Qué quieres decir?

Quiero decir que ella dijo que no debería, y que no funcionaría, y que ninguno de nosotros se va a mudar, y entonces por qué hacer más difícil decir adiós, o algo así. Creo que ella es algo evasiva.

O solo malentendiste la situación por completo.

O eso. Él se lo preguntó. No lo sé, aunque – hay algo en cómo me mira. Ella dijo ayer, bromeando, que estaba intentando convencerme de mudarme aquí para que yo pudiera verla cuando sea que quiera.

Ella suena un poquito loca.

Creo que ella lo está, y creo que me gusta eso. Pues, la gente aquí la quiere, así que ella no puede estar tan loca, ¿Verdad? La gente verdaderamente loca tiene dificultades manteniendo amistades sólidas.

Tú tienes dificultades manteniendo amistades sólidas.

Eres un dolor en el culo.

Ahí está ese elegante encanto de nuevo.

Lo digo en serio. No creo que ella esté realmente loca. Solo como, muy despreocupada, ¿Sabes? Como sea, ella también dijo que mi mano se vería bien en un anillo de boda.

Jesucristo.

Lo sé.

Y sientes lo mismo respecto a ella.

De verdad me gusta. Creo que la amo.

No le has... dicho eso, ¿O sí?

Una pausa.

Damian, no le habrás dicho que la amas.

Sí lo hice. Se me escapó mientras estábamos teniendo sexo.

Oh joder, estás perdido.

¡Cállate! Ella no se molestó. Dijo que piensa que la gente debería decir lo que está vivo en sus corazones, o algo así.

Ella está loca. Sabes qué, ustedes dos parecen perfectos el uno para el otro. Ella está loca, tú eres normalmente muy sensato. Pero ahora ella está volviéndote loco también, lo cual me parece la base de una gran relación.

Me ayudas tanto...

Como siempre.

¿Qué hago, entonces?

¿Me estás pidiendo consejo?

Desafortunadamente para mí, sí.

Bueno, creo que deberías venir a casa mañana y poner tu cabeza en orden. Siempre puedes volver. Si es real, lo que sientes que hay entre los dos, entonces será algo que tú podrás retomar, o mantener vivo por el celular o lo que sea. Entonces si aún sentís lo mismo el uno por el tras unas pocas semanas o meses o el tiempo que sea, puedes volver de visita. Tienes tiempo, ya sabes, para averiguarlo.

Ese es un muy buen consejo, de hecho.

Y dudabas de mí.

Nunca. Pues, sí.

Una pausa.

Damian.

Sí.

Estoy feliz por ti, hombre. Suena un poco loco, pero la vida es loca a veces.

Gracias.

Claro. Hey, mejor me voy. La cena está casi lista y los niños por poco se comen entre ellos si no les alimento.

No podemos permitir eso. Pequeños caníbales.

Gracias por llamar. Es bueno hablar contigo.

Gracias por hablar conmigo. Ha ayudado.

Bien.

Te quiero, hermano.

Yo también, nos vemos.

Él tocó el botón rojo y terminó la llamada, entonces puso su celular boca abajo en la mesa. Eran las siete en punto.

El Desenlace

Ella estaba pintándose las uñas de los pies cuando le escuchó llamar a la puerta. Exclamó que podía pasar y le dijo que estaba en su habitación. Ella escuchó la puerta abrirse y él le gritó al espacio, diciendo: Hola, ¿Interrumpo algo?

No, por supuesto que no, dijo ella. Estoy sola aquí y no puedo levantarme.

Él se preguntó qué rayos ella quería decir, y cuando él giró la esquina de la habitación él la vio sentada en el borde de la cama interminablemente enfocada en su tarea, su lengua asomando por un lado de su boca en concentración. Cuando la forma de él entró en su campo visual, ella levantó la vista y le sonrió brillantemente. Hola, tú, dijo ella.

Hola, dijo él.

Bésame.

Él lo hizo. Es un bello color, dijo él admirando sus dedos de los pies desde donde él estaba, junto a la cama. Combinan con esto.

Le mostró una flor trompeta amarilla que él había elegido en su camino hacia allí. ¿Para mí? Preguntó ella, mirándole a través de sus pestañas. Él asintió. Ella la olió y cerró los ojos por un momento, y entonces le preguntó si se la pondría detrás de la oreja. Él lo hizo, y ella se inclinó hacia él de nuevo para besarle.

Quiero hablar contigo sobre lo que estuvimos hablando antes, dijo ella.

Está bien, respondió él. He aclarado mi mente. Lo siento, me estaba quedando atrapado.

Oh, yo iba a decir que siento haber reaccionado tan mal a lo que era en realidad una idea muy normal. No normal como pensaría la mayoría de la gente, pero creo que dadas las circunstancias podría ha—

Él la besó de nuevo, y ella sonrió contra sus labios. Está bien, dijo él. Está bien, de verdad. Vamos a enfocarnos solo en esta noche.

Cuando él se echó hacia atrás él la encontró mirándole fijamente con algo que para él parecía admiración. Él guardó esta imagen en su mente y le rogó a Dios que él pudiera recordarlo justo como sucedió. Justo así, pensó él. De acuerdo, dijo ella.

Y vamos a fingir que me quedo para siempre. Pero es solo fingir. Él la miró directamente a los ojos. Solo fingir, dijo él de nuevo. Así que no te preocupes, ¿De acuerdo?

Ella continuó mirándole, la mitad de los dedos de su pie derecho pintados, la otra mitad no, y ella asintió muy solemne, sin romper el contacto visual. De acuerdo, dijo ella.

Él metió la mano en su bolsillo y sacó un barato anillo dorado de uno de los puestos de los vendedores ambulantes en la plaza y le dijo que ella podía ponérselo a él si ella quería.

¿Me estás pidiendo que finja casarme contigo? preguntó ella.

Exacto. ¿Qué me dices?

Lo haré, dijo ella, y ella tomó el anillo y lo puso en el dedo anular izquierdo de él. ¿Y qué me voy a poner yo? preguntó ella.

Él le mostró un anillo cómicamente grande con una gema de plástico, y se lo dio. Ella se rió en voz alta.

Es perfecto. Siempre he querido un gran anillo que le dijera a todos exactamente cuánto dinero tengo.

Sí es perfecto entonces, porque si de verdad nos fuéramos a casar probablemente terminaríamos siendo muy pobres con cómo arruinarías nuestra finanzas.

¡No lo haría! ella exclamó.

Siempre estás haciendo esto, dijo él insinuando una irritación casi creíble.

Siempre me han encantado nuestras discusiones de pareja, dijo ella entonces apoyando su cabeza en su antebrazo.

Mi amor, dijo él. Ella sonrió.

¿Cuánto tiempo más necesitas para estar lista? preguntó él.

No mucho. Solo terminaré estos pocos dedos y entonces me pondré ropa respetable y podemos irnos. ¿A dónde vamos, por cierto?

¿Te gusta la comida mediterránea?

¡Sí!

Bien, porque tenemos una reserva allí en quince minutos.

¿Dónde?

El lugar alto, se me olvidó cómo se llama.

Ella soltó una risita. ¿Alto Alto, sí?

Sí, eso es.

Bueno, ¿qué habrías hecho si no estuviera lista para salir?

Les dije en el celular que podríamos retrasarnos porque mi novia tarda mucho en estar lista. Así que ellos me dieron tres reservas para cada quince minutos comenzando con esta primera, en quince minutos.

Ella estaba sonriéndole incontrolablemente ahora.

¿Y si no me gustase la comida mediterránea?

Te hubiera llevado al restaurante italiano donde también tengo una reserva.

¿Solo una?

Sí, solo una allí, en treinta minutos.

Oh, ¿Y si no me gustase la comida italiana?

Entonces hubiera comido comida Mediterránea yo solo y te hubiera dejado disfrutar de tus gustos exquisitos en paz, pero sola.

Ella echó su cabeza hacia atrás, riéndose. Eres muy bueno conmigo, mi esposo.

Cualquier cosa para mi bella esposa. Dijo la palabra esposa en español.

Ahh, ¡Aprendiste una nueva palabra!

Él la besó en la cabeza y le dijo que la esperaría fuera.

¿No quieres mirarme mientras me visto?

No, dijo él mientras él salía de la habitación. Tenemos planes para cenar y no podemos permitirnos el retraso.

Pero sí podemos, dijo ella detrás de él. Porque dijiste que hiciste tres reservas.

No es educado, dijo él a través de la pared. Vamos.

Él pidió para ambos esta vez, y ella llevó puesto su ostentoso anillo toda la noche, y durante la cena ellos hablaron sobre el orfanato que él había buscado y lo que él había aprendido, y hablaron sobre la pobreza global y cómo las naciones más ricas parecían manejarla con increíble incompetencia, al menos respecto al gobierno, excepto por los países escandinavos, ella comentando que esos parecían hacerlo todo muy bien y ambos preguntándose qué era lo que tenían aquellos países que parecían prosperar entre los mismos retos de la codicia humana que aparentemente causaban que el resto del mundo se tambaleara.

Él dijo la palabra flounder en inglés, y ella no la conocía, y entonces él le explicó qué significaba y ella le dijo que era muy inteligente.

Realmente no lo soy, dijo él terminándose lo último de su bebida.

Lo eres, para mí. Sabías que anoche cuando estabas hablando sobre los derechos de agua y cosas así—

Ni siquiera pensé que estuvieras escuchándome, intervino él.

Sí lo estaba. Quiero decir que estaba distraída, pero era porque estaba pensando para mí lo inteligente y concienzudo que eres.

Pues, te casaste conmigo por una razón, respondió él, tocándole el muslo a través de sus pantalones de lino.

Así es, dijo ella, sonriendo. No puedo creer lo rápido que ha pasado el tiempo. Se siente como si solo nos hubiéramos conocido ayer.

Lo sé, cómo vuela el tiempo cuando se está enamorado.

¿Sí que me amas, entonces? Preguntó ella, mirando su rostro. ¿No has cambiado de idea con todos mis arrebatos?

Y él la miró y sonrió y dijo que por supuesto que no había cambiado de idea. Nunca he conocido a nadie como tú.

Yo tampoco, dijo ella.

Él no dijo que iba a añorarla. Él no le dijo que nunca la olvidaría. Esta noche estaba, él había decidido, fuera del tiempo y el espacio. Él no la añoraría, porque en el transcurso de esta noche él la tendría para siempre.

En sus ojos ella leyó el dolor que él sentía por amarla. Ella sintió cómo le conmovió. Y ella admiró su fuerza al construir esta noche para ambos a pesar de la manera en la que debía dolerle.

¿Podemos irnos a casa? preguntó ella entonces.

Él sonrió, amablemente, genuinamente, felizmente, pensó ella, y asintió. Entonces él pidió la cuenta.

Por la mañana ellos se despertaron sin alarma después de las

8:00 am y había llovido por la noche y ellos podían olerlo en el aire. Ella no fue a yoga, y él no se levantó para irse, y ellos se quedaron en la cama juntos durante toda la mañana. Después de que ellos hubieran hecho el amor, dulcemente, suavemente, silenciosamente, casi susurrando el uno al otro solo con sus cuerpos, sus pieles como secretos que cada uno guardaba para el otro, ella dijo desde su lugar apoyada en el pecho de él, que si se quedase, ella sería feliz.

Él se sintió sonriendo casi rebosando de emoción. Solo me quieres por el sexo, dijo él.

Mhmm, respondió ella. Es muy bueno.

Pero eso no es todo, añadió ella tras un momento.

Incluso mientras él sonrió, un conflicto de sentimiento surgió dentro de él. Podría haber sido que él encontraba difícil confiar en sus propios caprichos, dado que parecían estar cambiando siempre. Podría haber sido el sentimiento incómodo que llega cuando alguien está muy cerca de conseguir algo que quiere muy profundamente, como el dolor imperativo de tener y perder. O podría haber sido simplemente el conflicto entre el amor y la responsabilidad, sabiendo que aunque él quería quedarse, realísticamente no podía.

Sí que quiero quedarme, dijo él.

Entonces quédate. Puedes quedarte conmigo.

Él sintió esas palabras profundamente en su estómago.

No puedo, respondió él.

Lo sé, dijo ella entonces.

Pero puedo volver pronto.

Él sintió su sonrisa contra su pecho.

¿Cómo de pronto?

No lo sé. Quizá en un mes. Quizá antes. Hay vuelos directos. Quizá no pueda venir por una semana o así, pero podría venir para un fin de semana largo. Puedo hacer algo de mi trabajo aquí, en realidad.

No tenemos que tenerlo todo claro ahora, dijo ella suavemente. Tú volverás, y yo estaré aquí. Y entonces podremos casarnos de nuevo. Serás mi esposo americano.

Quédate aquí, ella le ordenó, levantándose de la cama.

Ella caminó suavemente sobre las pilas de ropa en el suelo hasta la estantería y sacó una antigua cámara Polaroid. Entonces ella se sentó otra vez a su lado en la cama. Haz como si me amaras, dijo ella, y tomó una fotografía antes de que él pudiera responder.

Él había estado mirándola, y ella a la cámara, ella sonriendo y él observándola como si ella fuera lo mejor que le podría pasar a él en el mundo.

Entonces ella le besó y tomó otra fotografía.

Ella le dio la cámara y le dijo que tomara una de ella sin ropa. Él lo hizo, y ella se negó a mirar la fotografía, pero él pensó que era la fotografía más bella de cualquier persona que él nunca hubiera visto. Él miró el reloj en el horno.

Mejor me voy, dijo él. Mi auto va a estar aquí en una hora y tengo que empacar.

¿Y si yo pudiera llevarte? preguntó ella.

¿Cómo, en la motocicleta? él se rió entre dientes.

No, por supuesto que no. Mi amiga Aditi tiene una camioneta y ella podía llevarnos a ambos al aeropuerto, yo podría volver con ella.

Él consideró esto por un minuto. Puedo pagarle por la gasolina y su tiempo, ofreció él.

Ella aceptaría con gusto dinero por la gasolina, pero ella no aceptará dinero por su tiempo.

Él sonrió. ¿Y quieres hacerlo? ¿A ella no le importará?

Me debe un favor o dos de todos modos, dijo Emilia, sonriendo. La emparejé con su esposo.

Ah, ¿Y ahora es su turno, eh?

Algo así, dijo ella, besándole en la boca y levantándose de la cama. Aunque no es lo mismo, dado que ya estamos casados.

Espera unos pocos minutos a que me ponga algo de ropa y los dos podemos ir a tu apartamento a empacar. Puedo ayudarte.

Oh no, dijo él. No me vas a ayudar a empacar. He visto tu armario. Eres un tornado. ¿Cómo se dice storm en español?

Ella lo miró entrecerrando los ojos, arrugando la nariz. Tormenta, dijo ella. La tormenta.

La Nota

Él no encontró la nota en su maleta hasta que puso su ropa para lavar después de llegar a casa. Era un pedazo de papel arrancado de su diario, fechado por un lado del día anterior con las palabras la tarde escritas al lado de la fecha. Estaba escrito en español. Por el otro lado había una nota en inglés.

Sujeta con un clip a la nota estaba la fotografía Polaroid que él había tomado de ella, y la de ambos besándose. Miró las fotos por un largo minuto, sintiendo las emociones más intensamente opuestas todas a la vez – dolor y alegría, pena y euforia, gratitud y resentimiento, miedo y esperanza – y entonces leyó la nota:

Quédate estas para que no te olvides de lo hermosa que soy. Escribí esta nota en mi diario sobre ti, pero vas a tener que mejorar tu español para leerla. ¡Nada de trampas! Llámame cuando llegues a casa. Te veré pronto.

Ella había escrito su número de celular debajo.

Para que no te olvides de lo hermosa que soy. Qué amenaza. Como si él fuera a olvidarlo alguna vez. Sería imposible. Imposible. Qué estás haciendo, pensó él para sí mismo, sonriendo sin reprimirse. Jesucristo. Jesucristo.

Agradecimientos

Esta traducción no sería posible sin la invaluable colaboración de Any Pascual, quien ha traducido esta historia al español con diligencia y delicadeza. Un agradecimiento muy especial a todos los que han contribuido en ayudar a que este libro se hiciera realidad, especialmente a Claire, María y Mackenzie por su primer feedback, y a Kiley por el increíble arte de portada que adorna la primera edición limitada en inglés. Me gustaría expresar mi agradecimiento a los muchos nuevos amigos que hice en México durante el viaje que inspiró esta historia, así como a mis padres, mi hermano, y mis hijos por su apoyo constante. Y por último, mi más sincero agradecimiento a todos los que habéis apoyado mi trabajo. Me habéis ayudado a llevar mis palabras por todo el mundo, y aún más importante, habéis creído en mí. Estoy eternamente en deuda con ustedes.

Acknowledgements

This translation would not be possible without the invaluable collaboration of Any Pascual, who dutifully and delicately rendered this story into Spanish. A very special thank you to everyone who had a hand in helping this book come to life, especially Claire, Maria and Mackenzie for your early feedback, and to Kiley for the incredible cover artwork that graces the Limited First Edition. I would like to recognize the many new friends I made in Mexico during the trip that inspired this story, as well as my parents, my brother, and my children for their perpetual support. And finally, my heartfelt gratitude goes out to all of you who have supported my work. You have helped carry my words around the world, and more importantly, you have believed in me. I am forever in your debt.

Sobre el autor

JP Greene es el autor de otros tres libros, incluyendo
el aclamado por la crítica Meet Me Between Breaths.
Nacido y criado en Colorado, Estados Unidos,
sus escritos han conectado con lectores de todo el
mundo, tocando su fibra sensible por su honestidad,
claridad y carga emocional. Es padre soltero, adicto
a las motos y entusiasta de la fotografía en analógica.
También es el fundador de la editorial literaria
independiente Tape Publishing, fundada en 2025.

Para saber más o pedir en línea más libros de JP,
entra en su página web
www.typewrittenlovenotes.com
o en su Instagram @typewrittenlovenotes

About the Author

JP Greene is the author of three other books, including the critically acclaimed Meet Me Between Breaths. Born and raised in Colorado, his writing has connected with readers around the world, striking a chord for its honesty, clarity, and emotional weight. He is a single father, motorcycle addict, and film photography enthusiast. He is also the founder of the independent literary imprint Tape Publishing, founded in 2025.

Learn more or order more of JP's books online at
www.typewrittenlovenotes.com
or on Instagram @typewrittenlovenotes

Sobre la traductora

Any Pascual es una poeta, traductora, bloguera, conferencista y persona altamente sensible española. Es una creadora cristiana, un alma cuyo propósito es amar, comprender y transmitir amor, y autora independiente de varios poemarios acogedores para almas sensibles disponibles en Amazon, incluyendo Sensibilidad: Los poemas de una Adolescente Altamente Sensible. Tormenta es su segunda novela traducida.

Puedes encontrarla en anayany.com, @any_espiritual en Instagram, Threads, X y TikTok, y @anyespiritual en Facebook y Bluesky.

Le encanta apoyar a otros autores, conectar con lectores y mantener conversaciones significativas con sus amigos así que, por favor, ¡Ponte en contacto con ella y di hola!

About the Translator

Any Pascual is a Spanish poet, translator, blogger, speaker, and Highly Sensitive Person. She is a Christian creative, a soul whose purpose is to love, understand and convey love, and the indie author of various cozy poetry books for sensitive souls available on Amazon, including Sensitivity: Poems of a Highly Sensitive Teenager. Tormenta is her second translated novel.

You can find her at anayany.com, @any_espiritual on Instagram, Threads, X and TikTok, and @ anyespiritual on Facebook and Bluesky.

She enjoys supporting other authors, connecting with fellow readers, and having meaningful conversations with her friends, so please, reach out and say hi!